Buckle My Shoe

To Lana,
Enjoy the story!
Roxanne was a
great encouragement
to me through the
writing process and
all that came
afterwards.

Buckle My Shoe

Maureen Flynn

PEMMICAN
PUBLICATIONS
INC.

Pemmican Publications gratefully acknowledges the assistance accorded to its
publishing program by the Manitoba Arts Council, the Province of Manitoba
– Department of Culture, Heritage and Tourism, Canada Council for the Arts
and Canadian Heritage – Canada Book Fund.

Printed and Bound in Canada.
First printing: 2013

Library and Archives Canada Cataloguing in Publication

Flynn, Maureen, 1960-, author
    Buckle my shoe / Maureen Flynn.

ISBN 978-1-894717-81-6 (pbk.)

    I. Title.

PS8611.L95B82 2013   C813'.6   C2013-904735-2

**PEMMICAN
PUBLICATIONS
INC.**

Committed to the promotion of Metis culture and heritage

150 Henry Avenue, Winnipeg, Manitoba
R3B 0J7 Canada
www.pemmicanpublications.ca

Canadian   Patrimoine
Heritage   canadien

Canada Council   Conseil des Arts
for the Arts   du Canada

MANITOBA ARTS COUNCIL
CONSEIL DES ARTS DU MANITOBA

Manitoba

MIX
Paper from
responsible sources
FSC   FSC® C016245
www.fsc.org

Dedicated to
Mary Ellen
John
Jillian
Patrick
& Joey

Prologue

Saturday, December 4, 1943

His hands were around her throat; he squeezed until the life had left her young body. She was only 16; he was 42. It was at this moment that Edith knew she would never leave Room 503.

He had attended to the task methodically, without emotion. He grimaced as he strangled her, yet his eyes only reflected detached indifference, as if he were performing a task as mundane as wringing out a facecloth.

When his work was complete, he started to leave, but hesitated. He turned and looked back at her lifeless body. Her pretty blue dress shimmered where the sunlight seeped in through a slit in the drawn curtains.

His steps were heavy as he returned to Edith's bedside. He looked down at her limp body. She was so young—too young for her life to be over. Still, he had no choice and no regrets. There was no other way. He knew that once his lies were revealed, she would have left him, returning to her parents and taking up with the first young man in uniform. He could not survive another rejection. In his mind, the truth was only masked by his deceptions.

He leaned over her and gently removed the gold watch from her thin wrist. He had bought it on credit. Next, he carefully unbuckled the new shoes she had been so proud of. The buckle was stiff and his fingers fumbled. The tightness of the new leather made them difficult to remove. He scowled as he pulled down hard at the heels then carefully slipped them off each of her lifeless feet. The radio was still on. It played, "There's No Tomorrow." How absurd, he thought. Carefully he pulled the blankets completely over her and left.

A silent scream of anguish froze heavy in Edith's throat. She was no longer on the bed, just above it. She wailed for the shoes he had taken, not for her life.

Chapter One

Monday, January 4, 2013

S teve Ascot woke with a start. Despite the coolness of the room, small beads of sweat had formed on his brow. His body was tense, unmoving. Only his eyes moved as he surveyed his surroundings. It was dark except for the morning rays that penetrated through the join of the drapes. Tiny dust specks floated in the air.

The whole room was unfamiliar and he struggled to grasp his presence. The transition from the terror of his dream to wakefulness was slow. It was the woman in the dream that troubled him, or was it a girl? What had she wanted? He tried hard to remember. He knew it was important somehow. She had been despondent, yet determined. He tried to recall her face, but he could summon only a vague recollection.

As he awoke more fully, his mind became alert. The dream began to fade and he remembered where he was. He also remembered what day it was and why he was here. He jumped out of the bed and headed straight to the bathroom, which was only a few steps away. He flicked on the light. The room was small for sure— even the tub looked half the size of what he was used to—but there were fresh white towels and tiny bars of soap wrapped in paper. It would do.

He turned on the shower and welcomed the sound of the pulsating water. It broke the heavy silence of the room. Stepping in, he was relieved to find that the water pressure was strong and it was hot. After letting the water spray over his face, he stood back, blinked and wiped the water from his eyes. He searched for his razor.

"Oh shit," he muttered, remembering that his razor was perched on the far side of the sink. He reached past the white plastic curtain and retrieved it.

Steve preferred to shave with a mirror, but he knew his face well enough to go without. He had a solid squared chin and a predominant straight nose. Someone had once said he had a Roman nose; unsure what that was, he decided to take it as a compliment. His skin was tanned and rugged from too many days on the beat, making him appear older than his actual age. His hair was thick and dark, with a slight wave, and bushy brows resided over his large hazel eyes. His one secret vanity was to pluck the hair between his brows.

Opening the small bar of shaving soap, he tried again to recall his dream. Her face would almost come into focus, and then retreat. He lathered the soap onto his face and began to shave. He concentrated on remembering her eyes. They were sad eyes.

"Knock, knock. Housekeeping!" called a distant voice.

Steve nicked himself with the razor and swore again. Blood dripped into the water, turning it pink. He grabbed a white facecloth and pressed it to his chin.

"Knock, knock. I must change the linens, please."

"Just a minute," Steve called. He grabbed a towel and wrapped it loosely around his waist. Dripping water and droplets of blood trailed behind him. He swung the door open and when he saw her, his annoyance faded. The maid's eyes bulged, her jaw dropped, and her olive skin had gone white to the lips. Realizing what a sight he must make, he laughed and watched her scoot down the hallway with her cart.

"I come back," she called over her shoulder.

Steve noticed her uniform was tight and her skirt was quite short. He closed the door, smiled to himself, and said aloud, "Looks like she seen a ghost."

He finished shaving at the sink, brushed his hair, and quickly cleaned the mess on the floor with the already bloodied towel. He put on his uniform, left his room and walked purposely down the hallway to the elevator.

His uniform fit well over his tall, lean body. He had run an iron over the cloth the night before, to give his image an edge, crisp and official. He thought the bulletproof vest was excessive for a security guard, but he wore it anyway to comply with the regulations. Only the slight stoop of his shoulders and the small piece of tissue stuck on his chin marred his otherwise impeccable appearance.

At the elevator doors, he pressed the down button and waited. He was on the fifth floor and considered taking the stairs, since he was now running later than planned. Before he could decide, the elevator arrived and the doors promptly opened. He entered and pressed Lobby.

Mirrored tiles lined the elevator walls. He wondered if this was deliberate to distract occupants who suffered from claustrophobia.

He peered with dismay at his many reflections. It was the tissue on his chin that concerned him. Quickly he pulled the tissue off, rolled it into a ball with his fingers and stuffed it into his pocket. He licked his finger, and putting his face close to one of the mirrored tiles, washed off any residual traces of blood.

The elevator stopped and he prepared to exit into the lobby. But number three was illuminated on the display. Glancing at his watch, he frowned and began to tap his fingers on his thigh. The doors opened. No one entered. He held the door open and leaned out, but nobody was waiting. He shook his head and pressed the door close button several times.

It was his first day on the job as hotel security at the Marlborough Hotel, and he did not want to be late. He was to report at 8. When the elevator doors finally opened, his watch read 7:55. He went directly to the front desk. Fleetingly, he wished he were in Toronto instead of Winnipeg; at least the first nerve-wracking hours of this crappy job would be over.

"Excuse me," he said.

Without looking at him, the young woman at the desk held up her index finger. "Shush."

She was peering intently into her paperback novel. Steve was in no mood to be shushed. Noticing a bell on the desk, he rang it three times.

She held her spot in the book with her finger and looked up, annoyed. However, when she saw Steve her face softened. There was something about him, she couldn't say for sure what it was but it was noticeable in an instant. A sort of contradiction, his commanding stature and rugged features didn't match the apprehension in his eyes. And his eyes were captivating, made you not want to look away, but she did. She held back a smile when she noticed the shaving nick on his chin. She handed him a tissue. "Do you know your chin is bleeding?"

He took the tissue she offered and nodded with a sheepish smile.

"You must be the new security guard. Steve, right? Well, you're not what I expected. I—"

Steve held up an index finger. "I'm sorry. I'm late and I need to report to Alec Kent."

"Well, aren't you something. I'm sorry too. I like to offer a bit of friendly chitchat, get to know people that way. You should try—"

"Please. Could you just tell Alec I'm here or tell me where I can find him. I'm in a bit of a rush."

She sighed and smiled in defeat. Steve noticed she had a nice smile, white, even teeth, and a small dimple on her left cheek. He began to regret his shortness with her, but did not have time to dwell on it.

"Please," he said, looking at her nametag. "Penny. I'm late now."

She picked up the phone and motioned for him to take a seat on one of the lobby chairs.

"Steven Ascot is waiting for you," she said into the phone, and went back to reading her book.

....

Steve waited. He was thankful, at least, for his surroundings, the beauty and spaciousness of the lobby helped relieve some of his anxiety. He had always loved the Marlborough, but a year ago he would have laughed at the thought of being an employee. Outside the streets were noisy with traffic and the sidewalks were dirty and messy from over-treaded snow and discarded cigarette butts. Walking through the hotel front doors was like entering another world, another time, a time when elegance and detail was highly regarded. Steve especially enjoyed the detail—the ornate plaster friezes, the carved, heavy-oak beams and especially the wrought iron light fixtures.

Without looking up from her book, Penny tapped the desk with her pen to get Steve's attention. It took a few times until he finally looked her way and she motioned to the pile of newspapers on the counter. Penny never looked up while he retrieved the paper. He was sure, though, that she peeked over at him a couple of times.

She was so engrossed in her book that Steve had plenty of time to get a full description of her. Out of habit, he detailed the facts: female, Caucasian, brown hair, green eyes, early 30s, thin, and fair-skinned with a hint of freckles. Gauging her height was impossible when she was sitting, but he estimated it to be between 5-2 and 5-4. Initially, he thought her green eyes must be enhanced by colour contacts. Then he dismissed the thought. She didn't strike him as the type to bother with contacts for no good reason. She had a pleasant face and was pretty enough. Not what most guys would consider hot, but still easy on the eyes.

Shifting in his seat, he began to concentrate on the headlines of the *Winnipeg Free Press*. He was drawn to the crime reports, out of habit, but reminded himself he no longer needed to be. Turning to the weather section, he noted it was -30 Celsius. With the windchill, it was -39.

He shivered as a gust of freezing air swept through the lobby. The attendant had been holding the doors open for an early arrival with lots of luggage.

A sturdy slap landed on his shoulder, nearly knocking him out of his chair. He turned and stood up abruptly, papers falling from his lap. Ignoring them, Steve extended his hand.

"Good morning, Alec. Steve Ascot. I was here right at 8…"

Alec ignored the handshake offer. "Yes, yes. I'm sure you were. I was just finishing off my breakfast."

Steve's face flushed as he picked up the scattered newspapers. He noticed Alec's shirt was partially untucked.

Alec nodded in Penny's direction. "Hope our shiny Penny hasn't been bothering you too much."

Penny ignored him and attempted to look busy, straightening papers and glancing at her computer monitor.

Alec walked toward the elevators. "C'mon Stevie. I'll show you around the old girl. She's quite a hotel."

This Steve already knew. Its grandeur was surpassed only by its history.

Alec walked confidently, almost with a swagger, arms swinging. He was not a tall man, but maintained a strong presence. The beginning of a paunch bellied over his belt buckle, but he would not yet be considered overweight. Muscular arms hung from sturdy shoulders. His limp blond hair was turning gray, and his hairline had begun to recede. His best quality was undoubtedly his wide smile and infectious laughter. It was what gave him his character and, at times, when he wanted, his charm.

The two men entered the elevator and Alec pressed nine. "May as well start at the top, work our way down, then stop for an early lunch. Maybe a few beer, eh?"

The elevator stopped on the third floor, but nobody joined them. Steve noticed Alec did not even wait, or look, to see if anyone got on. He just kept pressing the button until the door finally closed.

Steve considered that this maybe wasn't such a bad setup after all. How hard could security at a hotel be? He had a roof over his head plus early lunches, and a few beers with the boss to boot. Not too shabby.

"Sounds good to me, I'm starved, but didn't you say you just ate breakfast?"

Alec frowned and looked directly at him. "Rule number one, Stevie: mind the hotel security business, not mine!"

It was said without malice, but Steve knew Alec meant it. The elevator stopped again on the fifth floor and once again, nobody was waiting to get on. Alec repeatedly pressed the button, a little more impatiently this time. He's right, thought Steve. I have to learn to mind my own business. I am not a detective anymore.

He thought back to when he was. It was a tough job being a homicide detective, but he loved it, most of the time. There were some days he wished he could forget, days that haunted him. Horrific crime scenes, family's torn apart and grieving loved ones were the worst of it. Yet as much as it distressed him, it only compelled him to work harder, work smarter, to determine the killer and most importantly, get a conviction. This is the part he had loved; it was like solving a puzzle with many pieces, each piece critical in completing the picture. It was his exceptional attention to detail that made him a good detective; it was his perseverance and no-bullshit attitude that made him a great one. Steve sighed and reminded himself that his days on the force were done.

"Hey, dream boy. You coming?" Alec held the elevator door with his arm. "Can't secure the premises from la-la land." He laughed loudly and began walking away.

....

Their first destination was the Sky View Ballroom. As they headed toward it, Alec said, "So, Stevie, I'm dying to know. What does it take to knock a top Winnipeg police detective down to a security officer at the Marlborough? Must have been something big, eh?"

The question caught Steve off guard, and he felt his cheeks burn. "So what will my duties be here, exactly, Alec?"

Alec took the hint. "Well, if you can fix those goddamn elevators I'll give you a raise and kiss your skinny ass."

Alec laughed, and Steve was surprised to find himself laughing
too, possibly out of relief. "If there's going to be any ass-kissing,"
he said, "I'm sure I won't be on the receiving end."

They both laughed at that truth.

"I think I'm starting to like you, Stevie. Anyone who grasps the ass-
kissing order this quick must be OK. We should get along just fine."

Steve was feeling better. "I'll look into the elevator problem
this afternoon. Likely kids, or some prankster. I'll call the elevator company too. It must be annoying for the guests with all those
stops, not to mention the staff."

Alec nodded as he unlocked the double doors to the ballroom.
"Remind me to get you a set of keys after lunch."

A draft of cold air swept out of the ballroom as the doors were
pulled open. Steve shivered for the second time that day.

Alec began rambling on about the hotel. "This hotel, she sure is
a beauty of an old babe. Do you know it opened way back in 1914,
just before World War I? I never tire of it. Seems almost every day
I notice something new, a unique moulding or some stained glass
that I hadn't noticed before. Has had its share of celebrity too.
Even Winston Churchill dined here. Can't do much better than
old Winston can you, Stevie?"

Steve barely heard a word he said. He was in total awe of his
surroundings. He had been in this ballroom before, at a Christmas
banquet, but had never seen it as he saw it today, without the
crowds of people and the distraction of conversation.

The ballroom was enormous. Alec was saying how it could
accommodate 800 people. Steve looked up at the ceiling. It was
so expansive it made the tables appear miniature. He felt small as
well. Hanging from the beautiful ornate ceilings were several large,
glittering glass chandeliers. It was the windows, though, that gave
the room its true charm, as well as its name. So many windows,
and so large, with panoramic views of the Winnipeg skyline.

Steve walked through the maze of tables to one of the windows, where he stood looking through falling snow at the city spread before him. He felt a great sense of pride. This was his city—his old beat. It was truly beautiful.

The view he was taking in was pristine, innocent. It represented hope. Sure, he knew better. There was no scarcity of filth and crime and it seemed to get worse every year.

Alec stood beside him and broke the silence. "Quite a view, isn't she?"

As the tour continued, Steve was surprised to find an indoor pool and water slide on the premises. They skipped a few of the repetitive floors and ended back at the lobby by 10:30. Alec led him to the bar entrance and used his key to gain entry.

"Doesn't open till 11, but we can go in for a beer and wait," said Alec, then went behind the counter and grabbed a couple of cold ones from the fridge.

A tired barmaid sat at a table counting cash floats. She smiled briefly at Steve before continuing with her task. It was warm in the bar, and Steve took a long slow sip of his beer. This might work out after all, he thought.

Chapter Two

Steve had got through his first day at his new job. It had gone better than he had expected, but he was still relieved to retreat to his room after a light dinner in the café. His room wasn't much, but it was all he needed. It was in the older section of the hotel, and he liked its sparseness. The bed was wrought iron, of plain design, and was probably an antique. Thankfully the mattress was not, and Steve found it quite comfortable. There wasn't much else for furnishings, or room for them. A small dresser, an end table and a small chair were pretty much it. The room came at a good price for employees, and the cost was deducted right off his cheque. This suited him just fine.

Still in his uniform, Steve stretched out on the bed. A new job, a new place to live, and so many new faces—it was hard to absorb so much at once. He just wanted to be alone now. The TV was off for the moment, unusual for him. He usually welcomed the never-ending chatter and motion it supplied, but not tonight. The only light was from the small bedside lamp. Tired as he was, he had taken the time to position his shoes neatly by the door. Alone, his mind drifted back. Back to the same old question that had plagued him ever since that fateful day.

Was it self-defence or cold-blooded murder?

He ran over the details as he had so many times before. It was January 2012, a beauty of a day, sunny, no wind. It was cold of course, but -20 without the wind wasn't so bad.

Steve and a couple of the other detectives had just finished the breakfast platter at the Salisbury House on north Main. There were many Sals in the city, they were practically an institution, but the detectives only ever went to the one on the north end of Main Street. They'd been going there so long they felt at home and knew many of the staff and patrons by first name. Lingering over their coffee, they laughed at what Jill, their server had said just before she refilled their cups for the third time. What was it she had said? Oh yeah—*What can I get you? Coffee? Tea? Your coats?*

Well, it wasn't that funny. It could have been the unexpected balmy weather and the big breakfast that had put them all in a good mood. In addition, she always teased them about how long they sat around. When they finally left, they were still laughing and poking each other as they crossed the snow-covered parking lot to their unmarked gray sedan.

The youngest detective imitated their server, mimicking her high voice and pretending to puff up his hair. "Coffee? Tea? Your freaking coats?" The other two applauded his performance, then laughed harder when they saw her peering out the icy window. She was pretending to look insulted, giving them the finger and shaking her head. Then she smiled and dismissed them with a wave of her hand.

Just as they reached the car, Steve's cellphone rang. The other two detectives stood quietly while he took the call. It was brief. Winnipeg had suffered its first murder of 2012.

The three of them jumped in the car without speaking. Steve put the red cherry on the roof and they sped to the scene, down Main Street to an alley behind one of the hotels by Higgins Avenue. The patrol cars were already there, waiting for them. They got out of the car and walked at a fast clip to the taped-off area

Steve froze when he saw her. She was lying on her back on the cold snow in the alley. Her dark hair covered her face, but Steve knew exactly who she was from the fuzzy purple jacket that would never protect her from the cold again.

In the short time since the detectives had left Sals, the sky had clouded over and it had begun to snow. Large snowflakes drifted down on her. They sat softly on her hair and the fuzz of her jacket. Looking at her, Steve recalled a scene from The Wizard of Oz. It was the one where the falling snow awakens Dorothy and her friends from the wicked witch's spell. Only he knew this snow had no magic. She wasn't going to wake up, and she would not be making it home either.

What was her name? Cindy? No, it was Sidney, of course. He had arrested her for soliciting a few years back. Boy, was she pissed at him. She had been so young, and he had tried to play big brother, tried to help her get off the streets. Her response was to spit on the floor by his shoe. Steve figured she wanted to spit in his face instead, and he didn't blame her. Who was he to tell her what to do? What did he know about her life?

He told her to promise to take care of herself, be safe. If she ever changed her mind, he would help her out. He dropped his card close to where she had spit, and left heavy-hearted. After that, he would run into her now and then and would always wave and smile. Sidney would just spit on the sidewalk when he did this, but he was sure he caught her smiling afterwards a few times. She had been wearing the same fuzzy purple coat for the last few winters, so she was easy to spot. Now here she was.

Being sure not to disturb any possible evidence, he leaned over her and gently brushed the hair away from her face. Yes, it was Sidney, but not the Sidney he knew. This one had had the life knocked right out of her. Her face was still pretty despite the paleness and the large purple welt on the side of her head. She looked oddly serene, with almost a wry smile on her face, as if to say, *Better luck next time, big brother.*

Steve looked up to see a fire escape on the back wall of a three-storey brick apartment block, looming just above where she lay. Setting his emotions aside, he quickly attended to the business at hand. He commanded the officers at the scene to stay back and ensure no one came through the taped-off area without first being cleared by him. Then he instructed the other detectives to start knocking on doors in the vicinity to see if anyone had seen or heard anything. He knew this was futile—being a snitch in this neighbourhood was not healthy—but it was worth a shot, and the sooner the better. The forensic team and photographer arrived, and Steve watched over them as they worked. They knew their jobs well, but he wanted to be certain they took no shortcuts or missed anything, no matter how long it took or how cold they got. The job had to be done right.

One of the patrols handed him a hot, black cup of coffee and he took a big gulp, burning his tongue as he did. He always took milk and one sugar in his coffee, but he didn't even notice. A physical and emotional numbness had engulfed him, a coping mechanism that allowed him to remain professional and on task, no matter what. He was accustomed to the process; working a crime scene was no place for emotions to get in the way.

Some smart-aleck kid from a window above threw a snowball down at them. As Steve looked up to see which window it came from, he noticed a tuft of purple fuzz sticking to the metal fire escape. He pointed up and commanded, "Get some pictures of that first, from all angles, and then retrieve it for evidence."

Steve could no longer help Sidney in life, but he vowed to do everything he could to make sure her death—her murder—did not go unpunished. As it turned out, he wouldn't have to do much. One of the detectives sent to poll the neighbourhood had come up with a witness—an old guy who lived in the apartment block and had seen the whole thing. Said he usually kept his mouth shut and minded his own business, but he was getting old and getting tired, and couldn't take it anymore.

He said she'd been in an argument with a guy on the fire escape. He went to the window when he heard them yelling. He had opened his window a crack and heard her say, "I'm done. I'm leaving, and you can't stop me."

Turned out he could. The witness saw her spit in the guy's face, and then the guy raised his fist and punched her hard in the face, causing her to lean over the fire escape railing. Instead of helping her up, he lifted one of her legs and threw her over the railing. The old guy said it was a horrible sight, but she never screamed on the way down.

"I hope the wallop had knocked her out," he said, shaking his head.

From the old guy's description, Steve and the other detectives knew who it was right away—Jim Kobac, a mean son of a bitch and well known to them. As Jim put it, he took care of the ladies. What he meant was, he owned them, and they worked for him.

From the few times they had hauled Jim in, Steve had taken an instant dislike to him. Jim's head was shaved and he wore a bandana over it. He had a large nose that had seen a few breaks, and squinty eyes that were more like puffy red slits. He always wore dark glasses, and on the rare occasion he removed them, his eyes squinted and blinked like a mole emerging into the sunlight. His arms were covered in tattoos. They were evil-looking skulls and daggers, all in blue ink. Flamboyant rings covered most of his fingers. He wore an expensive tan leather jacket, no matter what the season, jeans and pointed black cowboy boots.

Steve was going to give orders to have Jim picked up, but decided to do it himself. He took a patrol officer with him. They checked a few of Jim's frequent watering holes, but he was not at any of them. As they drove down Main Street, on a hunch, Steve told the patrol officer to stop at a hotel they were just about to pass. The officer turned on the cruiser lights and parked at an angle out front. Steve got out and pushed through a group of smokers huddled outside the entrance. The beverage room had a few curious patrons staring at Steve and the officer as they made their way in. Sure enough, there was Jim, sitting at a slot machine. Steve knew it was him without him even turning around. Steve approached from behind and reached over the man's shoulder to press the cash-out button on the machine.

"What the hell—."

"You're going to have to come with us, Jim."

"The hell I am."

Jim swung a punch, but Steve was ready. Steve blocked the punch, grabbed his forearm and twisted it behind his back, dropping Jim to the floor.

"Are we going to need the cuffs today, Jim?"

He stood there while the officer read him his rights.

Jim's ticket cashed out at $98. Steve slammed the ticket on the bar. "Beers are on Jimmy," he said.

The officer escorted Jim out to the patrol car.

....

Pop! The bulb in the reading lamp in Steve's hotel room went black, ending his reverie. He pulled himself off the bed and turned on the main light. The memory of Sidney continued to weigh on him. The fact that she was finally ready to get away from the life she was living, only to have the life taken out of her. It just wasn't fair, and this was just one, one life lost. There were others he hadn't known and many who had no choice but to live a life that could be easily ended. But it was the image of Sidney, lying in the back alley with the snowflakes landing softly on her lifeless form in her fuzzy jacket, which got to him the most. He grabbed the remote, switched on the TV and lay heavy on the bed. With the remote still in his hand, he fell asleep before he could even decide what to watch.

Chapter Three

He awoke with a jolt. The room was like ice, yet he felt hot and sweaty. His breathing was laboured, and all his bedding, including the pillows, lay scattered on the floor. His eyes darted around the room. The only light was from the TV that still flashed pictures, creating shadows, illusions. He sensed someone was in the room with him. His instincts took over and he felt carefully for the remote. He pressed the off button, creating total darkness, and braced for an attack.

Nothing happened. He remembered he had been dreaming of the girl again. He had a vivid picture of her in his mind. She was just a girl, almost a woman, but not quite. She wore a powder blue dress, but no shoes. Her hair was dark and shiny. She had called him by his real name—Steven, not Steve.

A red light started flashing, lighting up the room with a glow. More fully awake, he realized he was alone. Any attacker would have made a move by now. Sitting up he felt dizzy, and he tried to steady his head with his shaky hands. He tried turning on the bedside lamp, forgetting the bulb had burned out. Nothing happened, but it made him realize that the flashing red light came from the phone beside it. He jumped when it began to ring. He reached to answer it and in his haste pulled it onto the floor. Grabbing the mouthpiece he blurted out, "Hello."

"Is this Steve Ascot, security?" asked a nervous voice.

"Yeah," he sighed, relieved to hear a voice on the other end. It diverted him from the dream and his abrupt awakening.

"Randall. Front desk. We got a lady stuck in the elevator."

"I'm coming," he said, and hung up.

He grabbed his pants and shirt and practically jumped into them. Slipping on his shoes without socks, he ran down the hallway, buttoning his shirt. He remembered he hadn't called the elevator people as he had planned.

"Shit," he muttered as he took the stairs two at a time to the lobby. He knew it was late, and a quick glance at his watch confirmed it was 2:45. In spite of the hour, he was surprised to find a small group of onlookers assembled in front of the elevators.

A woman was screaming from inside the elevator, "Get me out! It's so dark. Help me!"

Steve spotted Randall. "Have you called maintenance?"

Randall was relieved to see Steve taking charge. He could handle an unruly customer, or a late straggler from the bar, but an emergency of this proportion was not his forte. He had specifically chosen the night shift because it was usually quiet, with few people around and fewer disruptions. A woman wailing in a stuck elevator to a crowd of onlookers was too much.

"Maintenance is on the way, and I called the cops." Randall turned in the direction of the front desk.

"The cops? What the hell for? We just got a lady stuck in the elevator." The last thing he wanted was a run-in with any of his old co-workers.

Randall looked hurt. "Well, it sounded like someone was in there with her. It didn't sound good. I was worried."

Steve prayed the officers were not anyone he knew.

The wailing from the elevator continued. "Get away from me! Somebody help me, please."

Steve spotted the sleepy maintenance man sauntering toward them, crowbar in hand. He yelled toward the elevator, "Are you

OK? We'll get you out right away, miss. Is there someone in there with you?"

"Just get me out of here," was her only reply, and since Steve hadn't heard another voice he could only assume she was alone. He motioned with his arm for the small crowd to clear a path for the maintenance man.

Just then, two police officers burst through the front doors. They quickly surveyed the scene in the lobby and headed for the elevators, overtaking the maintenance man. They directed their questions to Steve, who despite his dishevelled appearance had an air of authority.

"What's the problem?" asked the taller one.

Steve was relieved to see they were young officers, and he didn't recognize either of them.

"No problem, really. Elevator's stuck. Our front desk clerk shouldn't have bothered you but he was—"

Sobbing sounds came from inside the elevator. "Help. Get her away from me."

The officers brushed past Steve, dismissing him. They positioned themselves directly in front of the elevator door. The taller of the two spoke into the closed doors.

"Calm down, miss. It's the police. You all right in there?"

The other officer added, "Is someone in there with you?"

Taken aback by the rookies' snub, Steve found himself amused at the comical sight of the two of them talking to a closed elevator door.

The panic and melodrama had gone out of the voice from inside the elevator.

"The police? Oh I'm OK. Just stuck in here. But it's awfully dark. Can you please get me out?"

"Are you alone in there?" one of them asked.

A sheepish "yes" was the response.

The maintenance man stepped forward. He pried the elevator doors apart with the crowbar. The elevator floor was two feet above the lobby floor. Steve and one of the officers held the doors open and the maintenance man shone his flashlight into the elevator, illuminating a pair of shapely legs.

The taller officer reached up and helped the young woman down. Her eyes were bulging as if in a state of shock, and she looked embarrassed. Steve did not recognize her immediately without her uniform, but it was the maid who had been at his door that morning. He felt sorry for her. She was not having a great day herself. Her dark black hair fell loosely past her shoulders, not tied back as it was earlier. Steve realized that it didn't take a shock to make her eyes so large, it was their natural state, and could probably be found quite captivating by some. She was petite, and Steve noticed again, she was quite shapely. She glanced at him briefly, and then smiled sweetly at the officers.

"Thanks so much for rescuing me," she said. "I apologize for my behaviour... well... all the yelling. I don't fare well in small places." She coyly tilted her head and melted them with her big brown eyes.

The officer shone the flashlight into the elevator, checking for another occupant.

The police had done nothing, Steve thought, but they were getting all her gratitude. No thanks to the real hero, the maintenance man. He let the elevators doors shut and then leaned a worn-looking 'out of order' sign against them. Then he shuffled away at a quicker pace than he had arrived. Randall had long since retreated behind the counter at the front desk. The crowd had dispersed, and Steve yawned and thought it might be a good time to make his own exit.

It was not to be.

"What the hell's going on here?" bellowed Mr. Kent, noticing the maid talking to the officers.

"Carla?"

Carla looked at Mr. Kent, then down at her shoes and did not look up again. The officers assured him everything was OK, the young lady was simply stuck in the elevator, but she was fine now. He suggested that Mr. Kent call first thing in the morning and get the elevator fixed before there was another incident.

"Thank you officers," Alec said. "Sorry to have bothered you tonight."

He gave them his best smile and a firm handshake each. Then he turned to Steve.

"Escort Miss Wright to her room," he ordered, "and be sure to call the elevator-repair people first thing in the morning."

Steve said nothing. He looked at Carla, motioned with a tilt of his head toward the stairwell, and waited for her to go first. Carla hesitated and looked at Mr. Kent, as if asking permission. A look and a nod sent her on her way. Steve held the door for her, and then followed her up the stairs. He noticed Carla did not just climb the stairs; she sashayed up them with a rhythmic sway of her ample buttocks.

Then, as if she had sensed him watching her, she stopped abruptly and turned.

"I can go on my own now," she said, with a knowing look. "You don't have to follow."

Steve gave her a big smile. "No problem, Carla. I'm having a wonderful time."

She glared and continued a bit faster, and with less of a swing to her hips.

"I wasn't alone in there, you know," she said over her shoulder. "Edith was there too."

"Who's Edith?"

"You don't know?"

"No. I haven't had the pleasure."

"Some security guard you are," she said.

They arrived at the fourth floor. Steve held the door for her and they proceeded down the hallway together.

"So, Carla, who's this Edith?"

She did not answer. "This is my room, thank you. Goodnight."

She opened her door quickly with her key, entered, and promptly shut the door in his face.

Chapter Four

Despite the early morning commotion, Steve arrived in the lobby at seven. He felt alert and well rested. After escorting Carla to her room, he had returned to his own and slept a deep, dreamless sleep.

The lobby was quiet, but showed signs of awakening to a new day. There was Penny, rushing behind the front desk, hanging up her coat. The front doors swung open as Randall left the hotel, his shift over. Steve wondered mildly what their lives were like outside of the hotel. Penny spotted him and waved. She was smiling and her eyes were alight. He hesitated; he was on his way to breakfast and didn't want to have to rush it. But it was only a brief hesitation. He did not want to repeat his abruptness of the day before.

"Morning Penny," he said. He rang the desk bell a few times for fun, and to let her know that he was in a bit of a rush again.

She beamed up at him. "What happened last night?"

"Well, I had dinner... watched a little TV..."

"Oh, come on. Randall said the police were called. Tell me everything."

"It wasn't a big deal, really. One of the staff was stuck in the elevator."

"Really? That's it? Why were the police called? Who was stuck in there?"

"Randall may have jumped the gun calling the cops, but he thought someone was in there with her. She was screaming bloody murder. I think he panicked."

"Yeah. Unless it's a bar fight or a drunkard, Randall's pretty useless. Who was it?"

"One of the housekeeping staff, Carla."

"Good grief! Wouldn't you know it? Carla! Randall says she's always roaming around at all hours. Where was Mr. Kent?"

"How does Randall know who's roaming around at night?"

"Security cameras, silly. Actually, you're the one supposed to monitor them, but don't worry. Between Randall and me, nothing goes on without us knowing. When I get tired of reading my books, I watch the tapes. They're almost as entertaining, sometimes more. Does Mr. Kent know about the elevator?"

"He showed up right when it was all over. I guess Randall called him, too, but he must have taken his time. He showed up looking very presentable for that time of night. He was very charming with the officers, but treated me like crap, then made me escort Carla back to her room."

"Oh," said Penny, and she winked.

"Are you kidding me? She slammed the door in my face. She did mention something that made me curious, though. She said Edith was in the elevator with her. Do you know who Edith is?"

Penny sucked in her breath fast and held it a moment while she covered her mouth with both hands. Then she stood up straight and ran her hands over her shirt as if to smooth it out. She pulled her book from her bag, and dismissed him with a wave of her hand. "Go on. I have to get to work."

Steve shrugged and grabbed a newspaper off the desk. Penny called after him, "Meet me at the bar at lunch. I'll tell you all about Edith."

....

Penny normally steered away from talk of ghosts. She supposed her fear would seem ridiculous to some, but to her it was very real. Especially with all the odd and unexplained happenings at the hotel! The stuff that went on around here was beyond any rational explanation. She refused to work the night shift and wondered how

Randall could do it. She preferred the bright of day and the hustle and bustle of the guests and staff. Yes, just the mere thought of ghosts gave her the jitters, but considering the circumstances, she figured Steve should at least hear about the ghost known as Edith.

....

Steve checked his watch; it was only 10 after seven. There was still time for a leisurely breakfast. First, though, he stopped at the pay phone and lifted the large phone book. He found the number for the elevator company, and then realized he could have got this information straight from the framed notice posted in the elevator itself. Oh well, he thought, maybe I'm losing my touch. He glanced at the number, committed it to memory and closed the book. His good memory had always served him well in his line of work. Or should he say his old line of work.

Arriving at the entrance to the café, he skimmed the front page of the paper while he waited to be seated. The first item that caught his eye was a picture of a couple skating on the river. The couple was holding hands and had frozen smiles on their faces. It reminded him that he had not gone outside the hotel in the past two days, and with good reason. Pausing to see if someone was coming to seat him, he noticed the sign that read, *Please Seat Yourself.* He headed toward a small table for two in the corner by a window.

He heard someone call his name. It was Alec. "Steve. Come join us."

Sitting across from Alec was an attractive blond woman. As she turned her head, a small diamond earring glittered playfully in the sunshine from the window. Alec pulled out a chair and motioned for him to come over and sit.

Steve was relieved to see that Alec was in a better mood than during their last encounter. He walked over to their table, but remained standing with his newspaper tucked under his arm. "I don't want to intrude," he said.

"Nonsense. Sit. This is my wife, Natalie." He seemed proud to introduce this lovely woman as his wife. Natalie looked to be in her mid-30s. Her blond hair was done in layered blunt cut and her pale blue eyes were framed with thick dark lashes. Any makeup was either expertly applied or non-existent, except for a hint of pink gloss on her lips. She wore a baby blue sweater set and designer jeans, and her shoes were flat loafers of obvious high quality. With a soft smile and a quiet voice she said, "You must be our new security guard, Steve. Welcome."

Steve took the chair Alec had pulled out. "Nice to meet you," he said and extended his hand.

"Likewise. And I apologize for my husband. I'm sure we're the ones intruding on your breakfast plans." She pointed politely to the paper still folded under his arm.

"Oh no," he lied, "I could use some company."

The smell of freshly brewed coffee filled the room, and Steve anxiously looked forward to his first cup of the day. He removed his paper from under his arm, and just as he went to place the paper on the white linen tablecloth, the server arrived to pour coffee. Newspaper and pot collided, slopping hot coffee over the table. A large splash landed on Alec's shirt. To Steve's relief, not a drop had the poor judgment to venture in Natalie's direction. Steve waited for Alec to react but to Steve's surprise, he never did. Alec simply asked the nervous server to bring a cloth, and dabbed at his shirt with his linen napkin. He was even smiling, which astounded Steve. His newspaper was now a dripping wet mess.

Completely ignoring the mishap, Natalie pointed to the coffee-soaked picture of skaters on the front page. "I used to figure skate," she said, "but that was a long time ago."

The server arrived, cleaned up as well as she could, and gave Steve a menu.

Steve turned to Alec and told him he had looked up the number for the elevator company and would call them right after breakfast.

"Great," said Alec. "So what are you having? The blueberry pancakes are—"

"Is there a problem with the elevators again?" asked Natalie.

Alec's neck turned pink, and his nostrils began to flare. Steve wondered why. And what was even odder was that Alec was still smiling. It was a forced smile, but a smile all the same. Steve regretted mentioning the elevator; it was obviously a subject of contention between the two. To help smooth things over he said, "It was nothing really. The elevator just got stuck between floors with a young woman in it. Maintenance had her out in a jiffy and she was fine. No big deal."

The server arrived and all were silent while Steve ordered hot oatmeal and a fruit cup.

"Good choice," said Alec, trying to move the conversation along, "That'll keep you warm on a day like today, but you really should try the—"

"Was it a guest?" Natalie persisted.

"No, Nat, it was just one of the staff. Nothing to worry about. Let it go."

"He's right, Natalie," said Steve. "Nothing to worry about. Carla was a little shook up, but she's fine."

Alec's neck grew redder and white spots were creeping in. He rubbed his temples as if to ward off a headache. He glared at Steve.

Natalie's soft voice became even softer, but Steve detected it held a strained patience.

"Carla, eh?" She stared at Alec. "I should have known. I thought you decided to let her go. And where were you when all this was going on?"

Steve decided to keep quiet. His oatmeal had arrived and it was steaming hot. He shoveled large spoonfuls into his mouth out of hunger and unease. A spoonful of cold melon soothed his burning tongue.

"Don't clam up now, Steve. Tell Nat I was there taking care of things."

Steve stopped chewing. "Well, sure he was. He came just after the police arrived and smoothed everything over just fine."

This time Natalie's tone was incredulous. "The police!" She clenched her fists, squeezed her eyes shut a moment, and took a deep breath. She lifted the napkin from her lap, folded it, and put it on the table. She stood angrily and left in a huff.

Steve and Alec sat awkwardly beside each other, facing no one on the other side of the table. After a few moments Alec rose.

"So nice of you to join us Steve," he said. He walked away quickly, as if hoping to catch up with Natalie and smooth things.

Pushing his food plates away, Steve put his elbows on the table and rested a cheek on the palm of his hand. Then he smiled and thought to himself, Mr. Kent is whipped, who would have thought?

The server, who had obviously heard everything, came by and silently cleared the table. She gave Steve a knowing wink as he got up to leave. Steve strode through the lobby and went to the front desk to grab a new paper. There were none. He would have asked Penny, but she wasn't at her desk, so he headed to the gift shop. He almost turned around when he saw Natalie in the shop, but it was too late, she had seen him come in. "Hi Natalie." At least she looked calmer and back to what he expected was her normal self.

"Oh hi, Steve, Sorry about breakfast; we shouldn't have been bickering in front of you."

"Oh no problem, it was nothing. I'd worry more if a couple didn't bicker."

Steve smiled, but Natalie sensed a troubled look in his eyes.

As he reached for a magazine on the rack, Natalie put her hand on top of his and looked closely into his eyes. Steve was amazed; this close, she was even more beautiful. Her skin was flawless and her face had an ethereal glow. "Don't worry, Steve. I have a knack for reading people, and it's obvious you are a good man. It'll all work out for you."

Her hand was still on his, yet he did not interpret it as flirtatious in any way. It was warm and caring, and it made him feel good.

"And don't worry about Alec; he's not as shallow and overbearing as he seems. Arrogant yes, but that's part of his charm."

Steve couldn't resist. "And Carla?"

Natalie's hand lifted off his, and she turned her eyes away. "That one... let me just say I don't have a good feeling about her."

He was sorry he had asked. As she walked out of the gift shop he called her name. She paused and looked back at him.

"Thanks," he said.

Chapter Five

Penny leaned over the table, locked her eyes on his, and in a low whisper announced, "Edith is a ghost."

Steve's eyes widened and his jaw dropped. He leaned closer to Penny and whispered back. "That explains so much. I've seen her."

Penny gasped, then held her breath, captivated. "You did!"

"It's true, I did."

Bang!

Poor Penny had never even noticed his hand rising until after he had slammed it down on the table. She nearly jumped out of her skin. Then she released an involuntary scream that echoed off the walls. It took her a moment to realize the scream had been her own.

Steve laughed so hard he could barely breathe. He certainly could not speak, and the look on Penny's face only made him laugh harder. He wiped a tear that was rolling down his cheek and tried without success to regain some sense of decorum.

Penny was furious. Not normally one to swear, she leaned over the table and slowly, but clearly, mouthed a single word: "asshole." This only provoked more laughter from Steve. It became infectious. Penny began to laugh, despite herself. Just when they were about done, Penny's drew in a few fast breaths, which caused her small freckled nose to produce an unladylike snort. Embarrassed, she looked around at the other bar patrons who were staring at them. At least they were smiling.

When Steve's cellphone rang, he could barely compose himself enough to answer. It was the elevator repairperson, who was waiting at the front desk. He hung up his cell and stood.

"Sorry Penny. Looks like you'll be dining alone," and added in a mysterious tone, ". . . or will you?" He walked away, smiling.

Now that Steve had gone, Penny turned to give the other bar patrons a stern look. It was her way of saying that the show was over. It worked. She retrieved a book from her bag and opened it at her bookmark. She settled in and proceded to bury herself in the book's medley of characters and charades, instead of her own. She found it difficult to concentrate, and her mind drifted to Steve and his audacious behaviour. She gazed at the same page for a long time.

Chapter Six

May 15, 1943

Edith was in a wonderful mood. She knew her life was taking a turn for the better. She was only 16, but felt very grown up. The past winter had been difficult for her, but spring had arrived and it was time to put it all behind her. She looked out the window and admired the new leaves sprouting on the large elm that stood just outside her third-floor bedroom window. In the cold of winter, the bare branches resembled the knurled fingers of an old woman. A strong north wind, and Edith's vivid imagination, would make the branch fingers appear to be reaching for her. Today, the brilliant new green leaves caressed her soul and beckoned her out. A robin landed on the branch outside her window. He tilted his head and one eye peered at her through the windowpane.

"It's officially spring; I've seen my first robin."

It wasn't just the spring air that had brought her out of her winter doldrums. She had decided to get a job and she was preparing to hit the pavement. She had washed and set her hair the night before, and it felt so good to take out the rollers she had slept in. She hated to sleep in rollers, but with no hair dryer it was the only way. One glimpse at the cascading curls in her mirrored reflection assured her that the discomfort had been well worth it. The sun filtered through the window and reflected off the mirror onto her dark auburn hair. The elm branches swaying from the breeze cast intermittent reflections of light and shadow, making her hair bounce and shine even more. After carefully applying her red lipstick, she blotted her lips with a tissue and then repeated the process. She smiled at her image and then frowned when she noticed a lipstick smudge on her front tooth. She quickly scrubbed it off with her finger. She dressed conservatively for the job interview, but her outfit did little to hide her blossoming beauty. She wore her baby blue cardigan with a grey skirt. The skirt had a wide flair that swished over her calves as she walked. She knew she was sure to be noticed by the young men passing her on the street.

Red lips smiling, hair bouncing, Edith set out. She knew exactly where she was going. Last weekend she had overheard a couple of girls talking. One was telling the other that they had heard Rae & Jerry's restaurant was looking for help. She knew it was her destiny, but she also knew she better get there before them.

As she walked to Portage Avenue she reflected on the past winter. It had been long and difficult for her. She had trouble with school. The trouble was she hated it, so much that she eventually just stopped going. She had thought this would end her discontent. She was wrong. Instead of enjoying being free to do whatever she wanted, she found there was not much she really wanted to do. She missed her classmates and even some of the teachers, and she just plain missed being part of something.

The worst of it, though, was her parents' reaction. At first, her mother tried everything to get her to go back, but it was no use. Edith would not budge. He mother eventually gave up and instead worried that Edith spent too much time alone in her room. When Edith did emerge, dressed for a night on the town, her mother was relieved.

Her father was another story. He was so mad with disappointment that he could hardly look at her. He barely spoke to her and when he did, it was perfunctory—"Set the table," or "Where's your mother?" This hurt Edith the most. She was so sorry for disappointing her parents. She had never really even considered how much it would affect them.

She had hoped that the disappointment her father felt was just his initial reaction. Surely time would soften his stance, but it didn't. What did change was Edith's reaction. Shame and guilt turned to contempt and rage. He knew nothing about her, he didn't understand her at all, didn't even try! She masked her anger with indifference. The two of them slipped into a routine of avoiding each other as much as possible and conversed almost entirely through her mother.

She had spent most of the winter months in her room listening to the radio. She barely went out, except for weekends, of course; one had to go out on the weekend.

She loved the excitement and the escape a night on the town offered. It granted her an essential respite from the mundane reality she endured at home, a tiresome and lonely reality that escalated over the long winter months. She yearned for the sounds of band music to fill her ears. She craved to feast her eyes on all the people chatting, laughing and twirling on the dance floor. Edith loved to dance and had ample opportunities. Out of breath after several fast dances, she would have to refuse some of the young men just to take a break and have a Coke. Icy cold, fizzy bubbles would cascade down her throat. It took her only a few moments to finish a bottle, and she was revived, ready to dance some more. The whole evening would make her dizzy with excitement and all her troubles would fade away.

Smiling at the memory, Edith continued walking briskly until her pace slowed as she passed the arched entrance of the building that housed one of her favorite millinery shops. The building was constructed of smooth-cut Tyndall stone that framed the two large windows on the main floor. Pausing to glance in the first window, she barely noticed her own reflection. Instead, she saw only the stylish hats on display. It took her back to a happier time. It was a quite few years back, yet she could remember clearly her father beaming proudly as he paid for a purchase at the register. The memory drifted over her, the sounds of the cash register, the towers of elaborate hat boxes and the smell of perfume lingering in the air. Her father had treated her mother to a new hat for Easter. It was the most beautiful hat Edith had ever seen, and she could not take her eyes off it, or her mother, who was equally beautiful. It was only when a woman reached from inside the store to replace a hat in the window display that her attention shifted.

She continued on her way and soon reached Portage Avenue. She headed west. The streets were bustling with activity, and she loved it. A streetcar honked at a pedestrian; Edith quickened her own pace. A stylish woman emerged from the hair salon and caught Edith staring, and then huffed and clipped her high heels in the opposite direction. Edith laughed. A young boy was carted off indignantly from the candy store doorway and Edith gave him an understanding smile. Swishing on her way, she seemingly ignored a raucous group of military men who hooted and hollered as she strode by.

It was a great day, and if she had to find any imperfection, it would have to be the discomfort of her shoes. They were too small; her toes had long since reached the end. They also had a few holes in the bottom. Her mother had cut out new cardboard liners, and that had helped somewhat. But it was not just the pain in her feet; it was the shame of the shoes' ghastly appearance. They were faded brown, scuffed, and no amount of polishing could return them to their original lustre.

Oh well, she thought, someday I'll have a brand new pair of shoes. First, she had to get the job at Rae and Jerry's. She knew it wasn't too much farther. She had been there once before, with one of the army men. He had taken her there for dinner, dazzling her. Most of her male acquaintances never even bought her an ice cream cone, let alone dinner at a fine restaurant.

The food was very good, like home cooking but better. She had ordered the pork chops and had finished both of them, as well as everything else on her plate. The man seemed pleased. She wondered if it was because she had not wasted any of the food he was paying for, or if he was thinking of the payment he would derive from her later. Either way she didn't care much; he would have received ample affections from her anyway. She could not resist a man in uniform. It was a weakness, she knew, but one she could handle. He had several drinks, and since she was too young to order her own, he had given her a few sips. After that night, she had never seen or heard from him again, but she relived the memory many times while lying in her room looking out the window.

So engrossed in her thoughts of her last visit, Edith nearly walked right past Rae and Jerry's. As she turned into their parking lot she was surprised to find all her earlier bravado had deserted her. Her lively pace had slowed almost to a complete stop. She wondered if they really were looking for help. If they were, why would they hire her? She had no experience, and she was likely too young. She was about to turn away when she saw the *Help Wanted* sign in the window. She walked hesitantly to the front door, slowly opened it, and entered. There was a large coat-check area and a reception desk. Both looked deserted.

She ventured farther and noticed that all the décor was very red, accented by dark panelling. There were many booths and tables. The place appeared dark and daunting. It didn't look like the lively, friendly place where she'd had dinner not so long ago.

An older lady in a starched red uniform with a white apron approached her. "Sorry dear. We're not open for several hours."

Edith's throat went dry. She somehow managed to ask about the job. "There's a help-wanted sign" she said and pointed to the window where it sat.

"Aren't you a little young to be working? Don't you have school, dear?"

Regaining her composure and realizing it was sink or swim, she took a deep breath and spoke with more conviction than she felt. "Oh no," she said. "I'm done school. I know I look young, everyone says so, but I'm actually 18. I could really use the job."

"Well... you look presentable enough. Any serving experience?"

"No, but I worked at Eaton's for a few months. They told me I was good with the customers."

The older waitress smiled and looked at Edith suspiciously. "What a coincidence. My sister works at Eaton's. In the china department. Maybe you know her?"

Edith looked down at her ugly, worn shoes. "No," she said.

"Well how do you know? I haven't even told you her name." Then she nodded knowingly. "Oh, I get it. No experience, huh? Well it's not all that hard. Come on, I'll show you around and get the boss to talk to you."

No one was more surprised than Edith when she landed the job. At first, she had only few hours a week, but when one of the full-time workers got married, Edith was given her shifts. Except for the trouble at home with her father, her life was pretty good. She loved her job and all her co-workers. When she wasn't at work she went out to dances, and any time at home was spent mostly in her room listening to the radio. Her favorite song was, *I'll Be Seeing You*, and whenever they played it, which was often, she would lie in her bed listening with her eyes shut. She always daydreamed about an imaginary soldier who was madly in love with her, kissing her goodbye before he left to serve his country.

She had a wonderful summer, but by the end of August Edith found living at home was becoming unbearable. Her father was home a lot due to a work injury and the tension was taking its toll on both her and her mother. One Friday night Edith and her mother quarrelled over the dishes. Edith was dressed to go out, and her mother claimed to be too tired and just couldn't wash up that night. Tempers flared when Edith refused, and it ended up with her walking out and slamming the door in her mother's face. The next day, she apologized and helped her all day, doing the wash and mopping the floors, anything that needed doing.

She had never quarreled with her mother before, and never wanted to again. It made her realize that it was time for her to move out. One of the ladies at work told her about a vacancy at a rooming house on Spence Street and she took it.

She was very excited until the events of moving day almost made her change her mind. Her father came in her room as she was packing and gruffly suggested she might want to take the radio with her. She hadn't dared asked, and never dreamed he would offer it to her. He tried to cover his kind gesture by saying they didn't play any good music anyway. What he did next nearly knocked her over: he gently patted her head and said, "You come home any time you want to."

Her mother hugged her, and wouldn't let go. Edith laughed and kissed her mother on the lips.

"I'm not far, and I'll visit lots."

Her mother finally released her grip and forced a smile, smoothed Edith's hair with her hand and said goodbye. Later, Edith's mother cried so hard that she gasped for breath. She was sick at heart and inconsolable. She had an overwhelming feeling that she would never see her daughter again.

Chapter Seven

May 26, 2013

The icy chill of another bitterly cold Winnipeg winter had passed. It had been a longer haul than usual. With June just around the corner, warm weather was surely on its way. Steve had spent the last few months mainly indoors at the hotel. His usually wind-burned face had turned pale. He went out only when he had to make a purchase, the first time being his mirror for the shower, followed by the occasional movie. Without realizing it, he had slipped into a comfortable routine at the Marlborough. Although he kept to himself much of the time, he had begun to cultivate a few friendships. Penny often joined him for lunch, and Randall had turned out to be a comfortable companion, too. Even Alec seemed OK most of the time, and Steve didn't mind spending time with him.

Randall was an interesting sort. He worked nights, because he had a young family—three kids under the age of five, two of them still in diapers. Seems the night shift was the only time he could catch any sleep. He was the only person Steve knew who could actually sleep with his eyes open. He would often sit motionless at the front desk with a pair of dark sunglasses slipping down his aristocratic nose. Steve found this amusing, and teased Randall about it, but never in front of Alec.

Randall was only five foot five, with dark skin and deep brown eyes. He had long black hair, which he wore in a perfect braid that reached his waist. Steve suspected that Randall's wife was the braider and imagined she enjoyed the process, a mental break from her motherly chores.

Randall was quiet and introspective most of the time, but he would share his lighter side with those he liked and trusted. His lighter side consisted of whispering jokes, rolling his eyes and poking others hard in the ribs. He liked Steve, so Steve often suffered from bruised ribs.

Randall had also discovered it could be great fun trying to play matchmaker, and was always coming up with new ways to entrap Steve into meeting single ladies. He was very creative. As much as Steve hated these games, he couldn't help but be amused at Randall's sheer enjoyment of the ludicrous circumstances he'd get Steve into. Randall would quantify his pranks by saying something like, "Hey, buddy, just trying to help you out. Don't see the ladies knocking down your door."

Despite it all, they had become friends.

During the winter months, their friendship reached beyond the walls of the Marlborough when a guest gave Randall a couple of free tickets to a Jets hockey game. He invited Steve to go. Steve liked hockey and accepted immediately. They were playing at the MTS Centre, which was only about a block from the hotel. They had a few beers and a burger at the bar in the hotel, and then walked over, arriving just before the game was about to begin. Their seats were great—centre ice, and only eight rows up.

Steve suffered a hard poke in the ribs just as an attractive woman edged past them on the way to her seat.

"Ouch!" Steve yelped, just as her backside went by him.

"Sorry" she said sweetly, thinking she had stepped on his foot. Randall held his breath trying to stifle his laughter. This time Steve rolled his eyes.

The puck dropped; the game started. Steve didn't like to miss a thing. He began to watch intently.

"So what do you think of Mr. Kent and his wife?" asked Randall.

"What?"

"Mr. Kent and the lovely Miss Natalie. What you think of them two? Quite a pair, huh?"

"Alec's OK, and his wife seems very nice. Why are you asking me this? Let's watch the game!"

"You do know her dad owned the hotel, before he died, shortly after their wedding?"

"Really?"

The buzzer sounded. The Jets had scored their first goal and Steve had missed it.

It became obvious that Randall was not a big hockey fan. After a few attempts to dissuade Randall from chatting, Steve finally gave up. From then on, Randall never shut up. After filling Steve in on the Kents, he moved on to Edith.

"She's a ghost," said Randall.

Steve grinned and this time he was poking Randall in the ribs, "Come on Randall, don't tell me you believe in ghosts too. I expect that from Penny, but not from you."

Randall grabbed Steve's wrist and held it firm, and with a more serious look than Steve had ever seen on his face he said, "Steve, it's true, I'm not kidding, Edith is a ghost! She was murdered in the hotel by some guy years ago. Now she haunts the place, especially the elevators, as I'm sure you noticed. I never take them, I only use the stairs."

Steve fidgeted uncomfortably and pulled his hand away. Despite Randall's sincerity he couldn't see any other way to react than to continue his ribbing, "Don't tell me you're afraid of ghosts, Randall," he said.

"Not scared, but I like to keep my distance. You should too, just in case they're a mean spirit."

"So is Edith a mean spirit, or a friendly ghost?" continued Steve still grinning, but with less bluster.

"Don't know, but she is a prankster. You've seen what she does with the elevators."

"Oh, come on, Randall. You can't believe some poor girl murdered years ago has anything to do with the elevators malfunctioning."

"What did the elevator repair guy say?"

"Said they were perfectly fine, just needed some maintenance."

"See what I mean? But they still make unscheduled stops."

Steve thought for a moment. "Well, you got me. Haunted it is. I'll put in a call to Ghostbusters first thing."

"Hey, it's not in your best interests to joke about ghosts," Randall said. "Oh and, don't mention any of this to Mr. Kent."

"Why?"

"He doesn't like anyone talking about the ghosts at the hotel. He claims it's bad for business, or at least the high-end business guests he's trying to attract. He says that if any guests ask about them, we're to smile and say..." Here, he raised his voice. "Yes, our resident ghosts are friendly and want to make sure all of our female guests have a comfortable stay and that all the men behave."

Steve laughed. "High-end business guests? Really?"

"Yeah, that's what Natalie expects. She also wants to add a spa to the hotel to attract them."

"So Natalie's father owned the hotel. And that's how Alec got the job as manager?"

"You bet. The job came with the marriage certificate."

"That explains a lot. Did you say ghosts, plural?"

"Lots in the basement, and someday I'll tell you about the old lady upstairs. Her piano disappeared about the same time as she did, but some claim to still hear it late at night."

Steve was no longer paying any attention to the game. "Tell me about that one," he said.

"I've said enough already Steve. All this talk is giving me the jitters and besides, are we here to watch the game, or tell ghost stories?"

Steve frowned. He glanced sideways at Randall, then smiled and shook his head. They both began watching the game. The Jets were now trailing by one goal. Steve began to watch intently again. Then Randall rose, said he'd go get them a beer.

....

Sometime later, Steve lay in his room and recalled the hockey game. He had just taken a shower and had spread a towel over his pillow to keep his wet hair off the pillowcase. He thought about what Randall had said. It was late May and although he now had a few friends here, he had decided to spend the evening alone in his room. He just wanted some time to relax and enjoy a little TV, maybe read a bit more of the book Penny had lent him. "Lent" was maybe too soft a term to describe how she had forced it on him and demanded he read it. She had just finished it herself and couldn't stop talking about it. When she noticed his eyes glazing over with boredom she decided he would have to read it too. That way he might show a little interest in what she had to say. She had pulled a book out of her bag and thrust it at him. It was about some little kid called Owen Meany. To tell the truth, he had quite enjoyed what he had read so far. Parts of it reminded him of his own childhood, carefree times spent with his brother.

Comfortable in his bed, he picked up the book and opened it to where he had stuck the napkin he used for a bookmark. He read a few pages, but found his mind wandered. When he realized he had no idea what he had just read he closed the book and flicked on the TV. That was no more engaging. He tried to settle in on an evening talk show, but he had no idea who the famous guest was, and their conversation was beginning to annoy him, so he muted the volume. He stretched and yawned and thought he might just fall asleep. Instead, his mind wandered and then rested on the conversation with Randall about the resident ghosts. He was surprised how serious Randall had become about it. He could tell the man really believed it. The more he thought about it, the quieter the room became. He reached over to turn on his satellite radio. It was one of the purchases that had required a rare trip outside the hotel. The voice on the radio filled the room. "… And when the night is new, I'll be looking at the moon, but I'll be seeing you…"

It wasn't his choice to listen to hits from the '40s, but his new radio always seemed to be tuned to the nostalgia station. After a while, the old tunes had grown on him. At times, the songs were sad and mellow, but more often they were snappy and uplifting. They offered lots of sax and piano, and the vocals always had a dreamy quality. He picked up the book again and the purring tunes in the background seemed to help him concentrate. He read about the little guy being up to bat and cracking the baseball smack into the beautiful head of his best friend's mother. He had not expected that! Steve reminded himself not to let on to Penny how much he was enjoying the book. In truth he found her bookishness rather endearing, and she did read some good literature. Mostly though, she poured over pocket romances or whodunits. She was addicted to them. He knew it was an addiction, because he'd often catch her hiding the front cover from him. Deception and denial, a sure sign, but he just laughed. She could be addicted to a lot worse.

A new song began on the radio. Steve lay the book face down on the bed and closed his eyes. Just as he was about to drift off to sleep a loud crash, from the bathroom, startled him wide awake. Knocking the book onto the floor, he jumped out of bed and went to investigate. Standing in the bathroom doorway, he felt an icy breeze pass by him. He held his breath a moment and then shivered. Turning on the light, not knowing what to expect, he was relieved to see it was just his shower mirror. It had slipped off the showerhead where he had balanced it and lay shattered into several pieces in the tub.

Too tired to clean it up properly right now, he decided to leave it and pick up the pieces in the morning. He went back to bed and noticed the radio had stopped playing. He looked around the room as if expecting to see somebody there. A door slammed shut in the hallway outside and made him jump. Jeez he thought, all Randall's spook talk must have got to him after all. He laughed at his jitters and remembered what his grandmother had always told him: "Fear the living, not the dead!" He concluded that he must have nudged the power button on the radio when he got up.

....

Putting all thoughts out of his head, Steve lay motionless on his bed and concentrated only on falling asleep. As he was slipping off to sleep he heard the radio come back on, or was it? The sound of piano music filled his room. It was a beautiful melody and hauntingly familiar. As hard as he tried, he couldn't rationalize where it could be coming from. No one had a piano in their room for sure, and he knew there were no performances scheduled at the hotel. Even if there were, they would be located far from where he could hear from his room. It got louder as the melody progressed, and for a moment Steve found himself literally frozen in fear. He decided it must be another nightmare. The lovely melody continued, but was played more tenderly. It drifted slowly off into the distance.

The music had lulled him to a sound sleep. His body was still. Only his mind continued to churn, processing the day's events, his subconscious cleaning the cobwebs of his conscious mind. At first his dreams were unfocussed—Alec and Randall playing hockey, or was it Steve himself with his brother? They were on an outdoor rink and it began to snow. Next thing he knew he was running. It was hard to run in his skates. He came to an alley and was now skating fast, he shifted his weight and turned and stopped. At his feet was a girl, just lying there. She wore a purple fuzzy jacket and bare feet. He didn't know who she was so he knelt down and as he reached to brush her hair from her face he suddenly remembered. Sidney! Her face was still bruised, but as the snow stopped falling the bruise disappeared—and her face changed. The purple jacket faded, revealing a pretty blue dress. He was afraid. He began to get up, but he was slipping on his skates. Next thing he knew, he was back in his room, and the girl was lying next to him on his bed. She turned her head to face him and her eyes popped open and glared at him. Loud, disturbing piano music echoed in his head until he could take no more—his own eyes opened and he lay rigid in his bed. He jumped up and went in the washroom and threw some cold water on his face. He flicked the volume up on the TV and went back to bed.

Chapter Eight

"Let's go to the beach."

"Now?"

"Yeah. I love to go this time of year, before everyone else."

"But it's raining."

"Just a bit. It'll stop."

"I only go to the beach when it's sunny."

It was only the end of May, not quite beach time in Manitoba, not this year anyway. Penny was trying to talk Steve into a drive to the beach.

It was a Monday, both their days off. Steve hadn't expected to see Penny. Now here she was on the phone trying to get him to go to the beach, of all things. He wondered at her motive. Well, it might do him good to get out of the hotel, out of the city. He loved to look at the lake, and the sky always seemed bigger out in the country.

"OK, when?"

"Really?"

Steve thought she sounded awful surprised. He concluded she must have expected more of a fight. She probably had some convincing lines prepared and was disappointed not to have the chance to use them.

"Now," she said. "I'm downstairs."

"Well, give a guy a few minutes to shave his legs."

"I'll be in the lobby, smart ass. Hurry!"

To speed things up, he skipped the shower ritual since he had taken one the evening before. A quick birdbath, as he called it, and a thorough brushing of his teeth were all he allowed himself. He could have used a shave, but thought, to hell with it, it's my day off and I'm going to the beach. He did take his time dressing. It wasn't often he was out of uniform, and he wanted to choose carefully. Finally, he decided on a pair of beige shorts with a black golf shirt that had the same beige trim on the collar as the shorts. He touched both up with the iron. Then he slipped on his black sandals for the first time that year, grabbed his wallet and a windbreaker, and he left his room. He usually took the stairs—to keep fit, he told himself—but decided to ride the elevator today. It arrived quickly, and he smiled politely at an attractive older woman who was headed down. The elevator stopped at the second floor, and he moved aside to allow her to exit. She did not get off and no one got on, either. She smiled at him. He pressed 'L' for the lobby several times, then the elevator started down again and they arrived at the main floor.

Penny was waiting for him. "What took you?"

"Had to have a shower," he lied.

"Hmm, your hair dries fast. Should have opted for a shave instead."

"Never mind, Agatha Christie. How are we getting to the beach?"

"I borrowed my Mom's car."

"You can drive?"

"Just because I take buses everywhere doesn't mean I don't know how to drive."

....

It was Randall's one day to cover the day shift so Penny could take the time off. He raised his eyebrows in exaggeration a couple of times as Steve and Penny whisked by. Steve was sure he heard him humming 'here comes the bride' as they left. Jerk, he thought, and then laughed.

Standing outside Penny asked, "Are you laughing at my car?"

Steve looked at the tiny red, rusted Pony. "Nope. The car makes me want to cry, not laugh."

"Oh, get in," Penny said.

....

She manoeuvered through city traffic like a pro. It started to rain, and she turned the wipers on. Steve gave her a sideways glance, as if to say I told you so.

She was undeterred, and turned up the radio very loud. It was early, and the popular morning-show DJs were still bantering. They were discussing how hockey players first started wearing 'the cup,' or jock straps, in the late 1800s, but they never wore helmets until the 1970s. The DJs joked about how it took the men a hundred years to figure out it might be important to protect their heads as well. Penny gave Steve a sideways glance.

Steve put a fake scared look on his face, hunched his shoulders, and covered his crotch with both hands cupped. Penny cuffed him lightly in the head.

Assured of Penny's driving abilities, Steve put his seat back, partly to get some distance between his knees and his face in the little car, and partly just to relax. He had not planned to fall asleep, but he did.

....

"Honk, honk."

Steve woke with a start and banged his head on the roof of the car.

"What the hell?"

Penny smiled at him. "We're here."

He couldn't believe he had slept all the way. It was about an hour's drive to Gimli, a small town on the shores of Lake Winnipeg. Penny had already found a parking spot. Steve rolled down his window and a waft of fresh lake air seeped into the car, replacing the last breaths of the stale city. His eyes squinted as he stepped out of the car and he reached back in to retrieve his sunglasses. There was no sign of the rain they had encountered earlier, and the bright sun warmed his skin. It was early in the season so he was surprised to see so many people out on the streets. Except for a young couple that ran by him, most of the pedestrians were taking their time, taking in the sights. From where he stood he could already see the harbour. It housed a large smattering of vessels from small sailboats to luxurious yachts. They appeared to sway in slow unison. His peaceful reflection was interrupted by the loud squawks of a couple of seagulls arguing over ownership of a deserted Cheesie under a bench.

He looked over at Penny as she hurriedly fumbled with something in the trunk. He couldn't help but notice her tight-fitting top and low-slung jean cutoffs. It was not her usual state of dress, but he decided he could sure get used to it. As she stood and slammed the trunk shut he saw it! Propped on her head was the most awful oversized plaid hat.

She caught him staring at her. "I know," she said, "but I have to wear a hat in the sun. Need to keep the freckles at bay."

She was standing on the sidewalk by the car. She retrieved some sunscreen from her book bag and started rubbing it vigorously onto her face and neck.

"Want some?"

"No thanks," he said, smiling to himself.

He neglected to tell her there was a big white splotch of lotion on her nose that hadn't been rubbed in. Instead, he asked her if she had a camera. She said she did, and pulled one out of her book bag. He wondered if there was anything she didn't carry in that bag. He had her stand by the car and snapped her photo. She protested, but posed and smiled anyway.

"Let me see it," she said.

"Later, I'm starved," he said, and slid the camera back in her bag. "Me too, where do you want to have lunch?"

"Last time I was here I had a good burger at a place called Grrrumpy's. It's just down the street by the hotel."

"When were you last here? Grrrumpy's closed a few years ago, I think there's still one in Selkirk, though. My husband used to belong to a book club that met there."

"Your what!"

"My husband. Don't look so damn awkward. I should have said my ex-husband, but yeah, believe it or not, I was once married."

Steve couldn't have been more surprised. He had never really thought about Penny in a relationship with someone else. Married—he hadn't considered that.

....

They stopped to pick up a couple of orders of fish and chips from a roadside stand, and headed straight to a bench by the shoreline. Penny relaxed as they sat eating and looking out at the lake. She talked about how her parents used to bring her and her sister to Gimli for a whole week every summer. They rented a cabin about a block from the lake and she told him how she loved to ride her bike. How she rode to her heart's content, discovering every inch of the beautiful lake town. "Such a nice change for a kid from the city," she said.

She went on about her precious summer memories—bonfires with marshmallows, Scrabble games in the cabin and cuddling tight to her mom while her dad told frightening ghost stories.

Steve listened intently. He liked imagining her as a young girl, happy and carefree. Even though she had once been married, he still found her very much a young, innocent girl. He felt an overwhelming need to protect her from the brutalities that life sometimes offered.

As if reading his mind, Penny got up from the bench and began running toward the water.

"Come on!" she yelled.

He shook his head and wondered what she was doing. Then he saw them. Just down the beach, about a hundred or more seagulls were pecking away at something on the sand. Penny kept running toward them.

Steve pulled out the camera and snapped her photo as she chased the seagulls. She had caught them off guard, and they all took flight at once. It was something to see them flapping away, proclaiming their displeasure in loud, shrill squawking. Penny's hat had fallen off and she had kicked off her shoes to gain speed. She slipped and fell on her rear end, laughing the whole time. Steve snapped another shot.

Steve checked the photos; all were keepers. He slipped the camera back in her bag and hoped she hadn't seen him. He noticed two bottles of wine in her bag and wondered at that. Penny returned to the bench, breathless and laughing. Then she felt a bit guilty and flung her remaining fries out to the seagulls. The birds besieged them immediately, and she imagined she was forgiven.

Penny was having a great time. Still, she hadn't forgotten the purpose of the trip. After a walk on the pier and a bit of browsing in the shops, she herded Steve into the car and drove to a secluded part of the beach. She parked the car and grabbed a blanket and her book bag. She waved him out of the car to come with her.

It was a very small stretch of beach, cluttered with driftwood and an uprooted tree. The waves were lapping on the rocks, but it was sheltered from most of the wind that had picked up. There were still a few ice patches on the lake, and Steve was thankful to be in a sheltered spot. He grabbed his jacket, which was hanging from the back of the passenger seat. Penny spread out the blanket and motioned for him to sit down beside her.

"Be gentle with me," he teased.

"Oh, shut up. At least we won't get arrested here," she said.

"Arrested! Sounds even more intriguing."

Ignoring him, she pulled out a bottle of wine and two plastic glasses out of her book bag and quickly unscrewed the cap on the wine. She poured herself a small glass, and then filled his nearly to the rim.

"Trying to get me drunk now? Is this what you learn in all those romance novels you read?"

Concerned that he'd seen through her, she gave him the small glass and took the full one herself. "This one's mine."

They sat quietly for a while and looked out at the lake. Then Steve, feeling very relaxed, lay on his back, clasped his hands behind his head, and shut his eyes.

Penny figured she better move the conversation along before he fell asleep again. She decided to start with a fairly safe subject.

"Are you and Carla... well... you know... are you?"

He smiled. "Would you be jealous?"

"Me? Why?" Penny's cheeks flared red. She was either blushing or her sunscreen wasn't doing the job.

"Isn't that why you're asking? I'm beginning to get a lot of vibes from you, taking me out to a secluded beach..."

He laughed as she threw a book at his stomach.

"Listen, I'm trying to be your friend," she said. "I'm not positive, but I'm almost convinced that Mr. Kent and Carla have something going. I wouldn't want you losing another job."

Steve looked forlorn. Penny regretted her last words; the wine was already loosening her tongue. It was supposed to be loosening Steve's, not hers!

"Sorry," she said, softly.

Steve snapped out of it. "Well, you can rest assured that Miss Carla won't give me the time of day, and I don't mind one bit. She may be pleasant enough to look at, but she smells funny. Have you noticed?"

Penny took a large gulp of her wine. "Vinegar," she said.

"You don't like the wine?"

"No, Carla smells like vinegar. Get this. She's a maid, right? A maid who is allergic to cleaning supplies! Well maybe not allergic, but sensitive to them, she claims. She does all her cleaning with a blend of vinegar and water. She doesn't get a regular paycheque either; her envelope on payday is always cash in an envelope. I don't know where she's from, but I bet she's not supposed to be here."

Penny was just getting started. Steve lay back on the blanket again and looked up at the sky, so big. While he listened to her he noticed a dark cloud heading their way.

"Her first payday, she comes to ask me how to do a money order. I explained and showed her where the post office was. I see her go there every payday."

"Sounds like she might have family back home who can use the money. Probably doesn't have a visa to work here. I wouldn't condemn her for that."

"Oh, me neither. I actually don't mind her, except if she's having an affair with Mr. Kent. Poor Natalie just lost her father a few years back, right after the wedding. She doesn't need any more heartache."

"What makes you think they're having an affair?"

"Well, it's the knowing glances, and you know him, he flirts with all the female staff. Correction—all females. It's harmless, but I've never seen him flirt with Carla."

"That's it?"

"Well, I see certain comings and goings in the hotel, the security cameras, you know. By the way, I've seen you giving her some hard up-and-down looks, and glancing over your shoulder a bit too long after you pass her in the hallway."

"So, shoot me."

Steve poured her another glass of wine and tipped his into the sand. "You're a bit of a sleuth, aren't you?" he said, and she nodded.

"When I'm not reading my books I run the security tapes from the night before. It's usually boring watching empty hallways, but if you're patient, you see some very interesting things."

"I bet you do."

Penny's plan was failing miserably. She was doing all the talking. But the more wine she drank, the more she talked. Having brought up the subject earlier, she even began to tell him about her husband. She told him how she was only 21 when they married, and how she was sure it was true love forever. She thought she had found her life mate, the father of her children-to-be. How she had been blissfully happy making a home for them.

"What happened?"

She didn't say anything for a while and they sat silently while she continued to pour herself another glass of wine and then another. She grabbed a tissue and blew her nose and then started talking again. She told Steve how her husband and cheated on her. How a well-intentioned friend had told her and how she had hated her for it.

"At first I was sure she was lying, just trying to cause trouble. I even suspected she wanted my husband for herself."

Steve passed her a fresh tissue. She motioned her glass for a refill and he hesitantly obliged.

"At least he never lied when I finally asked him... I almost wished he had."

Penny took a large sip and then began to cry quietly. Steve put an arm around her shoulder and she rested her head on his chest.

"He said she didn't mean anything to him," she sniffed. "Was that supposed to make me feel better? He broke my heart for someone who meant nothing! He tried everything to win me back, but I was done."

She sat up straight and retrieved the second bottle from her bag. Unable to unscrew the cap she passed it to Steve. He hesitated, knowing she'd had enough, but relented at the sight of her teary eyes and her outstretched arm dangling her glass. He refilled his too, but only took a few small sips; he knew he was now the driver of the rusty red Pony.

"I don't know why...I don't know why I'm even telling you this."

She closed her eyes a moment then opened them and rested her head back on his chest.

"We got a divorce and I was done. No more. I meant it Steve, you believe me, right?" She didn't wait for an answer. "Then I met Gregg. He was so good to me, treated me like a queen. It took me a really long time, a long time, but I trusted him. I really did! He was so good. I told him all about my husband, what a liar and cheat he was. Gregg hated him, really hated him, because of me, Steve."

Steve was getting worried she was saying too much and hoped she wouldn't regret it. He wanted to put an end to it, but she kept going on and on. It seemed she needed to vent, to release these sad memories. The least he could do was to listen. Plus, he had to admit his curiosity was getting the best of him.

"I never thought I'd be happy again Steve, but Gregg was the best. I never had to worry about him being unfaithful. He had good morals, Steve... good morals!"

Penny took a big, laboured breath, followed by a long, slow gulp of wine.

"You won't believe want happened next, you just won't."

He knew for sure now that she had, and was going to, say too much. She went on between sips and sniffles and told him how, after a while, Gregg developed a wandering eye. She said she had pointed it out one time and he had said, what did it matter where a man got his appetite so long as he came home to eat? She told Steve she had asked Gregg what would happen if he got so hungry that he couldn't make it home in time. How Gregg got mean and told her she was just paranoid after the trouble with her husband. How he told her it wasn't going to work out between them if she didn't trust him, so she had hid her jealousies and suspicions.

Steve was sorry when she told him that one night Greg did get very hungry and didn't come home to eat, didn't come home until the next morning.

"Oh Steve, it hurt so much and I was so mad. I even struck out at him, scratched his face. That made him really mad and he blamed me for everything."

Steve passed her yet another tissue.

"He said it was because I was so damn boring in bed. That's what he said, Steve! Said it was always the same old thing, lights out, under the covers. I thought that's what he wanted! Then tells me he wanted, *needed* more. Why didn't he tell me...?"

Steve wasn't sure if an answer was expected, but before he could decide she wailed, "He even said he hated my flannel pajamas! I thought he loved those pajamas!"

Steve was ready for another outburst of tears, but instead she gave him a little push and they both fell back onto the sand. He was relieved to hear her laughing. Laughing uncontrollably, but laughing just the same. He smiled at the thought of her in her flannels and was just about to join in when her laughter reverted back to sobs.

"Shush, shush." He stroked her hair. It seemed to calm her a bit.

It made Steve angry the way these men had treated her. He couldn't listen anymore. Besides, Penny was way beyond tipsy and didn't look well.

"That's it," he said. "Time to go, Penny."

He found the car keys in her bag and helped her into the front seat. Once he made sure she was strapped in, he collected the wine bottles. The second one was still half-full and he emptied it into the sand. He grabbed her bag and the blanket and put them with the bottles in the back seat. He barely got in the driver's seat when the rain started to come down.

Penny sat quietly in her seat as he pulled the car out of town and headed down Highway 8, back to the city. He relaxed his shoulders against the back of the seat and was just settling in for the drive home when he noticed her holding a hand over her mouth.

"Uh, oh."

He quickly pulled onto the shoulder, reached across her to open her door, and released her seatbelt. None too soon, she leaned over and retched on the gravel.

He passed her the whole box of tissue from the back seat and looked away as she blew her nose several times. Her hair was now wet from the rain.

"Thorry," she said, "I never drank. Take me home."

It was only then that it occurred to him that he had no idea where her home was. He figured he'd worry about that when they got closer to the city. For now he just wanted to get there. But after only a few minutes on the road, she announced that she had to pee. Again, he pulled over, and not trusting to leave her out there alone he stood by her while she went. He was a gentleman and kept his eyes averted the whole time. They were both pretty drenched now from the rain. Once she was back in the car he helped her buckle her seatbelt, then drove off, praying for no more stops.

Penny was feeling a bit better now and looked up at Steve. In her glazed outlook she was sure her plan was going tremendously well. He looked fuzzy, which meant he must be drunk by now. She worried that he was driving, but it was too difficult to figure what to do about it. Instead, she blurted out the question she had been dying to ask. "Whadja leave yer ol' job fer?"

Steve was not expecting this question. After a long pause, he decided to answer truthfully.

"I killed a man and I'm not so sure it was self-defense."

He looked at her to see her reaction.

There was none; she was sound asleep.

Chapter Nine

September 15, 1943

Summer had slipped by and Edith was sad that the leaves had begun to turn. She did not dwell on it, though; she was too happy, happier than she had been in a long time. The window in her room was propped open with a small piece of wood. Sounds from the street drifted in while she prepared herself for work. She heard a motorcar pass, and then the young girl who lived on the ground floor apartment. As usual, she was skipping and singing.

"One, two, buckle my shoe. Three, four, shut the door," floated up from the sidewalk. When Edith was outside, the young girl would often coax her to skip with her by singing, "One, two, three, sugar by the sea. I call Edith in to tea."

Edith liked the young girl and often accommodated her invitation to tea by skipping along with her. But not when she was with Albert. He would have thought she was acting like a kid. Albert was much older than she was, in his forties she figured, although he would never say. He was definitely not the dreamboat man she fantasized about meeting, although she did like the fact that he had been in the army.

Once he had shown her a photo of himself in uniform. It was old and blurry, but she could tell he must have been a handsome soldier. In the photo he did look a bit like her dream boy might, so that is how she imagined him to be.

In the beginning, she would just seem to bump into him on the street—too often to be a coincidence, she later realized. He would smile shyly at her and tip his hat. Finally, she spoke to him one blustery day. "Quite a wind, sir. You'd best hold onto that hat."

He said nothing, just smiled and scurried off. At the time, she had been struggling to hold her skirt from blowing up in the wind. She couldn't help but notice him leering at her, likely hoping she would prove unsuccessful.

Eventually they started chatting when they met on the street or on the main floor of the rooming house. Usually their conversation was about the weather or some other mundane topic. This progressed to longer conversations, and often they would sit on the stoop of the rooming house until late into the evening.

Edith told him all about how she had left school, and she was pleased that he understood and never asked if she planned to go back. She talked about her job and the people she worked with. He cautioned her to not become too friendly or tell them too much. *Keep to yourself,* he advised; *it's for the best.*

....

Over a short time they became very close, and Edith began to depend on him for his friendship and guidance. He treated her like a princess, and even bought her a gold Gruen Tara wristwatch. He must be well off, she thought. Of course, she realized it was a bit of a bribe; she was no dumb cookie.

After their friendship had progressed, he began demanding that she stop going to her Saturday night dances. She was stubborn, and besides she loved the dances and all the men in uniform who went to them. She wanted to go, and he was not going to stop her.

Albert had finally realized she would not listen, so he tried another tactic. He arrived at her door one Saturday night, just as she was slipping on her shoes to head out to another night of dancing. At first, she was angry when he walked in, assuming he was there to try and stop her from going out, but then she saw the small box he was holding.

"What's that?"

"It's for you, dear."

She opened the box to find the gold watch. She never went to the dance that night, or any night after.

Chapter 10

They were still making their way back to the city. Steve drove while Penny slept. When she began to snore, Steve turned up the radio.

The day at the beach was not what he had imagined. The fact that she had once been married was the biggest shocker of the day. That, and the way she hit the bottle. He forced the other sad tales she had told him out of his head. They made him too angry.

The rain had been pitter-pattering most of the way, but now it was coming down in a white spray. The flimsy windshield wipers were no match for it. Earlier, he had opened his window a tiny crack for some fresh air. Now the rain was coming down so hard, even with the window open that little bit it was blowing in and drenching him. He closed it tight with the hand crank. The windows began to fog. They cleared quickly when he turned on the defrost. The rain became louder and louder as it pounded on the roof. Steve glanced over at Penny and thought what a lonely sound a heavy rain could be. He turned the radio up some more.

It was still daylight yet the sky had turned very dark. The only light was from the occasional bolt of lightning that had started. The loud cracks of thunder only made Penny squirm and change her position for comfort. He was surprised when after one loud crack she leaned towards him, held his arm, and rested her head on his shoulder. At first, he felt uncomfortable and wondered whether he should try to reposition her. The next crack of thunder solved his dilemma as she shifted again.

Steve concentrated on his driving. His shoulders were hunched and his head was lowered close to the windshield as he tried to keep his gaze on the road. He considered pulling over at one point, but dismissed the idea, not relishing the thought of sitting on the side of the highway. He'd rather get back.

The radio announcer rattled on about how the last five months in Manitoba had been the coldest in 16 years. Rub it in, Steve thought. Then, to twist the knife some more, the announcer added, "In 1988, I was just a young man of 18 then, don't do the math, ha, ha. But friends, in 1988, today's temperature was 34 degrees C."

Steve switched the station. The new one was reporting that a plane had gone missing en route from Brazil to Paris. They suspected the plane might have been hit by lightning.

Steve shut the radio off. He had always held a high regard for all human life and hated to hear of disasters like that. He knew all too well the heartache felt by so many when just one death occurs. It was difficult for him to fathom the magnitude of mourning that would follow such a large disaster.

It had been his mother who had taught him how valuable each person was, no matter what their circumstance. She was driven to help the needy, almost obsessively. He and his brother Jake would tease her as she ran out to work at the soup kitchen in the north end of the city.

"It's okay, Ma. We'll get our own lunch. Don't you worry about us."

She would just laugh and blow them both kisses and run off. He missed her terribly and never really got over the fact that she was gone. His one relief was that she was not alive to know he had killed a man. Had he killed a man? Well, yes, he had, but the tireless question lingered—was it murder or self-defence?

Steve's mind wandered back to the arrest of Jim Kobac at the bar. He had decided to ride in the patrol car with the officer and the suspect. Jim looked up at him and laughed as the officer assisted him into the back seat of the car. "You got nothin' on me. I'll be back at the bar by suppertime."

"How about an eyewitness? That work for you, Jim?"

Jim's face had changed. He flung himself onto his back in the patrol car and came out full force, landing both his boots in the officer's gullet. The momentum and the element of surprise thrust the officer backwards and he plowed into Steve, knocking him over. Jim fled on foot. Steve scrambled up and pursued him. Steve was fast, and determined.

Jim had assumed he was far enough ahead to duck into a pawnshop. Steve rounded a corner just in time to catch a glimpse of Jim's tan jacket before the door flung shut. Steve entered the shop carefully, gun drawn.

"C-c-can I h-help you?" said the young man minding the store from behind the counter.

"Where is he?"

The clerk said, "Who?" but as he said it he motioned with his eyes, indicating the back of the store.

"Never mind," said Steve and motioned with his head for the clerk to exit out the front door. The man readily complied. The bell on the door jingled as he left.

"Thanks. You played it smart kid," said Jim as he emerged from the shadows of the storeroom.

Steve was standing behind the counter, gun pointed at Jim.

Jim smiled, trying to appear relaxed and in control, but he jumped when Steve's cell rang.

"Ascot here," he said, never taking his eyes or the barrel of his gun off Jim.

It was the other detective.

"Bad news. Our eyewitness caved in, said he was pretty drunk, could have been dreaming it all."

"Good to know," Steve said. "I have a little incident here. Bing's Pawn Shop on Main. Send some uniforms."

He hung up and looked at Jim. "And maybe an ambulance."

Steve wanted to shoot him before the others arrived. With the witness out of it, he knew Jim likely would be back at the hotel for supper, and who would be his next victim?

As much as he wanted to shoot Jim in cold blood, he knew he couldn't. It was not in him to take another life, even knowing what the future might hold.

As far as Jim knew, they still had a witness and he'd probably be going away for a long time. That and the fact that back up was on the way, made Jim very dangerous, and Steve knew it. Steve also knew that he alone stood in his way.

Jim was the first to speak, "I guess we just wait now, huh? Hope they hurry. I'd like to get this little misunderstanding cleared up. All that running has made me hungry and I'm already thinking what I want for supper. Too bad the lovely Sidney won't be joining me tonight." He frowned maliciously, and then he laughed.

Steve was furious; he could literally see red. "Bread and water for supper tonight, Jim. I told you we have an eyewitness."

"Yeah, that won't last. That jerk will surely see the benefits of a retraction."

Steve's cell rang again.

Jim lunged headfirst over the counter, aiming for Steve's gut.

After that, Steve didn't remember anything, not even pulling the trigger. All he could remember was seeing Sidney's beautiful face, smiling.

The officers burst in just as the shot rang out. They assumed both men were dead. Both were covered with blood, and both had their eyes wide open—Jim's staring wildly, Steve's with a look of calm.

....

A car honking jolted Steve from his thoughts. He realized they were back in the city and could barely remember driving the last stretch of highway. The nut job behind him kept honking, and now he was getting out of his car and coming towards Steve's window. He looked mad. It was then that he noticed he was stopped at a green light at the intersection. Not one to turn down a confrontation, Steve grabbed the door handle ready to get out. Penny shifted in her seat, still sound asleep.

Maybe he'd better give this guy a break today. Just as the guy showed up at his door, he pressed the auto door locks, smiled, waved at the guy through his closed window, and took off.

Steve watched the guy in his rearview mirror. The man was trying to get into his car to pursue him, but the light had turned red again and cars sped in front of him from left to right.

Steve turned to Penny. "Wake up!"

There was no response. He gave her a nudge. "Come on, Penny. I don't even know where you live. Wake up."

Nothing. After several more attempts to wake her, Steve decided he'd have to take her back to the hotel. She should likely sober up a bit before going home to her parents.

When they arrived at the hotel, he realized there was no way he could risk going through the front doors and lobby, for her sake. If Randall were still on duty, Penny would never live it down. Randall would tease her about it forever.

He parked in the lane behind the hotel and sneaked her through the side door. She could clean herself up and have some coffee. Then he'd drive her home.

Chapter 11

The plan had a few flaws. Penny would barely wake up, and he had to practically carry her up the five flights of stairs. He was also sure he saw Randall, nose pressed to the window, when they scooted into the lane. The rusty red Pony stood out from the other cars on the road.

Now, here she was, sound asleep on his bed. He covered her with a blanket and took her shoes off for her. Sitting in the chair, he weighed what to do next. A growl from his stomach answered him. Deciding Penny would sleep for a while yet, he decided to go to the bar for a quick bite.

He usually took the stairs these days, but after five flights up with Penny, he chose to take the elevator. It made its usual unscheduled stops, but he barely noticed. He got out in the lobby and there was Randall, smirking and raising his eyebrows up and down.

"Coming up for air?" He laughed.

"Shut up," said Steve.

Randall put both hands in front of his mouth. Next, he covered both eyes with his hands, and then his ears; their secret was safe with him. Steve figured it was, and then remembered there was no secret; Penny just had too much wine and needed to sleep it off. Ignoring Randall, he walked into the bar. Alec was there, finishing a beer and ordering another. He spotted Steve and waved him over. Steve decided he'd better get his food to go.

"Where you been all day?" said Alec, slurring his words. "Come have a beer."

Alec wasn't drunk, Steve decided, just nearing the end of the day and he'd likely had a few since lunchtime. He drank often, but Steve had never seen him really drunk.

"Well, a quick one. I'm just getting some supper to take to my room."

The server had overheard and brought Steve his usual brand of beer and a glass that she first checked to make sure there were no spots. She had become accustomed to Steve's fussiness. She also brought him a menu. Not sure if Penny would be able to eat, he ordered two burgers to go, just in case.

"Hungry, or do you have company?" said Alec.

"Hungry," said Steve, and then realized this offered an opportunity. "There's something I've been meaning to ask you, Alec, but I know how you hate me minding your business."

"Go for it, Stevie. If I don't like the question, I just won't answer."

"It's about Carla."

Alec's face lost some of its colour.

"What about her?"

"She's quite a looker."

"That she is," said Alec and took a slow last sip of his beer.

"Is there something going on between you too?"

Steve regretted saying it the moment it came out.

"You gotta be kidding," Alec said. "Have you met Natalie...? Well, to be honest it is tempting. Carla has made some blatant offers, but alas, I'm a one-woman man."

Alec held both hands to his heart, fluttered his eyelashes and then laughed. Steve didn't pursue the interrogation. If Alec was having an affair with Carla, he wasn't going to admit it, and there was still a slight possibility he was telling the truth.

Alec, however, continued to talk. He told Steve that when he and Nat got married, her father had insisted on a prenuptial.

"Nat didn't think it was necessary, but she always did what Daddy said. I didn't want one, made me look like a fool. I was truly in love with her, not her Dad's money or the hotel. But, I went along. Anyway, the old man kicks off shortly after the wedding and leaves the hotel to Natalie. I love this hotel, Steve. Except for marrying Nat, it's the best thing that's come my way. Do I sound like a guy in a position to cheat on his wife?"

The server brought Steve his burgers.

"No, I guess not," said Steve.

"So go for it, take your best shot with her. Good luck, though. I think you'll need it."

"Good luck with what?" asked Natalie, who just arrived. Steve quickly pulled a chair out for her.

"Just an idea I had for fixing the elevator," said Steve, covering quickly. Then he made a quick exit.

As he walked away, he overheard Nat and Alec arguing about a banquet on the ninth floor. She wanted him to check on things, but Alec was happy where he was. The beers had kicked in and made him brave.

"Go check on it yourself for once," said Alec.

Steve could imagine the look of disdain on Natalie's face. Glad to get away he took the stairs, two at a time, to the fifth floor. The lights had flickered in the stairwell a few times and he figured the storm must be getting worse. He stopped at the drink machine to buy a couple of canned drinks. Just as the second drink fell, he heard a scream from the direction of his room. Dropping everything, he raced down the hallway and ran into Penny.

"Are you crazy!" yelled Penny.

"Was that you who screamed?" he asked.

Penny nodded.

He held her tenderly and smoothed her hair. She lifted her knee into a most tender spot.

"Are YOU crazy?" he said pushing her away and holding the tender area with both hands.

"Where's my car, I've got to go."

She hadn't kneed him too terribly hard, but it had hurt just the same. Somewhat recovered he said, "We'll get you home. Are you going in bare feet?"

Penny looked down to see she had no shoes on. Steve was picking up the drinks and the bag of burgers.

"Come on back in the room. And don't worry. I'll be a perfect gentlemen, even though you've proven not to be much of a lady."

"I'm not going back in that room!"

Hungry and impatient, Steve just walked towards the room without her. "Don't then."

Considering her options for a moment, she decided to follow him rather than to be left alone in the hallway. Steve was sitting in the chair, eating his burger. Penny stood in the doorway, looking around as if she expected to see someone pop out. The radio was playing hits from the 40s, as usual.

"You like 40s tunes do you?" said Steve, smirking.

"That freakin' radio came on by all itself, after the lights went out," blurted Penny.

Taking the last bite of his burger, Steve wiped his mouth carefully with a napkin. "So that's what all your screaming was about. It's just the storm, you know."

"Just a storm! I don't think so. This room spooks me out. I don't know how you can stay in here."

Steve noticed she was trembling.

"I think someone has a bad case of the jitters. Could it be from her overindulgence this afternoon? I gotta hand it to you Penny. You can put 'em back."

"You don't know anything, and you're a bit of an ass," she said.

"Oh my, listen to the language. I would have never suspected it. Here I thought you were more of a bookworm, the drab little front-desk girl. Boy was I wrong. Turns out you're a wine-guzzling party girl."

"Oh shut up. I was trying to get you drunk. I've never been drunk like that in my whole life! Do you even know whose bloody room this is?"

"Uh, yeah, mine."

She whispered softly and mentioned Edith only for the second time since he'd known her "It's Edith's room," she whispered. "It's the room she was murdered in."

Even though Steve did not believe in ghosts, he realized this information could explain the dreams he was having. The girl in his dreams must be her. Leave it to Alec to give him this room. He wondered why no one had told him. He rationalized that he must have overheard someone say it was Edith's room and he had just forgotten. His subconscious hadn't, hence the dreams.

"Well, I hope she doesn't mind my company then," said Steve, dismissing further discussion about it. "Why don't you have a shower and I'll drive you home. You can tell me all about why you wanted to get me drunk. Good plan kid, too bad, it backfired on you, eh! By the way, where is home? I'd have taken you there in the first place if I'd known."

"Oh my God—the car! I told them I'd have it back before supper. They'll be worried sick."

"You better call them and let them know you'll drop it off in about an hour."

"Why would I drop it off? I live there."

"OK, whatever. Get showered and we'll go. Do you want a burger?"

"No. And I don't need a shower. I'm not going to shower in your room, especially with you here."

"Trust me, you need a shower. You want I should leave?"

Catching a glimpse of herself in the mirror she had to agree. She needed to get cleaned up before going home. But she sure wasn't going to be left in here alone again.

"No! I mean yes, I'll shower, but you stay here."

She pulled a chair close to the outside of the bathroom door and motioned for him to sit. "Don't go anywhere, and keep talking to me while I'm in there."

She flicked on the bathroom light, entered, and looked at Steve one last time before she shut the door. Steve grabbed the second burger and lay on the bed. He couldn't help but imagine her in there removing her clothes. He dismissed the thought out of decency and took a bite of the burger. He remembered he was supposed to be talking to her.

"You OK?" he asked, a mouthful of burger muffling his voice.

"Yeah."

Trying to come up with some conversation he said, "You have nice green eyes, you know."

There was a pause. "I know."

"Are they colour contacts?"

"No!"

"I didn't think so."

He heard the shower water come on and figured he could quit talking for a bit. He closed his eyes a moment just to rest them. He hoped she was OK. He knew she was still feeling the effects of the alcohol. At least he hoped that was the case after the knee in the crotch. He hoped that wasn't something she would normally do.

A loud scream sounded from the other side of the bathroom door. Steve opened his eyes and leaped out of the bed.

"What happened?"

He wasn't sure if she was just scared again or if something had really happened. He decided not to take any chances and pushed open the door. She hadn't locked it. The first thing he saw was the blood. Her naked body dripping wet, she stood on one foot and leaned on one arm resting on the back of the toilet. Blood was spurting from the big toe of the foot she held up. She was a pitiful sight, with tears streaming down both her cheeks.

It didn't take Steve more than a second to realize what had happened.

"Fuck," he said. The broken mirror. He had forgotten all about it.

He eased her down until she was sitting on the toilet. He gently held up the injured foot. It looked bad with all the blood, but he couldn't be sure how deeply it had been cut. Manoeuvering her so she was facing the shower, he held her foot under the running shower a moment and once some of the blood washed away he could clearly see the piece of glass still sticking in her toe. It was a large piece and he decided it would be best left in until he could get her to Emergency at the Health Sciences Centre.

Remembering his first aid, her wrapped a facecloth around the glass and then wrapped a towel around her entire foot. Grabbing the first thing he could find, he picked her bra off the floor and wrapped it around the towel to secure it in place. She'd likely need a few stitches.

Penny looked woozy, and he was afraid she was going to pass out. He filled a water glass with cold water and threw it in her face. She opened her eyes wide and realized she was still very naked. She blushed and tried to cover herself with her hands.

Then the lights went out. The storm outside was still raging. Penny was not scared this time. Steve was right there with her. She was more concerned about her bleeding toe and welcomed the small dignity the darkness allowed her.

"Oh great," said Steve. How was he going to get her out of there and over to the hospital in the pitch dark?

Before he could come up with a plan, the lights came back on. He grabbed his large white terry robe off the hook on the door and helped her put it on. She balanced on her one good foot as she slipped her arms into each armhole. Steve wrapped it around her tightly and tied the belt in a knot. Once again, he lifted her into his arms and carried her out of the room. The blood was soaking through the towel and was dripping on the floor. It left a trail behind them. No longer caring what anyone might think, he sat her in the large wing chair by the elevator and pressed the down button.

The display above the elevator showed that the elevator was stopped on the ninth floor. It stopped again at the eighth floor, then the seventh. Steve could hear the lightning storm raging outside and wondered how long the power would stay on. He knew it was risky to take the elevator with the power switching on and off, but at this point, he didn't think he could manage to carry her down the stairs. He questioned his decision when the power went off twice again just in the time they were waiting for the elevator to arrive. Penny was quiet, sitting in the chair. He was worried about her and wanted her to keep awake.

"It's almost here. You OK?"

A groggy, "What?"

"You OK, Penny?"

"Never been better."

He was relieved she hadn't lost her sarcasm.

Finally, the elevator doors opened.

Thinking back on the events later, Steve would recall how slowly the doors had seemed to open. After they did, it was as if time stood still. The first thing he noticed was the blood. There was much more this time. It was splattered everywhere. The second thing he noticed was the glitter from a small diamond on an earlobe of the elevator's lone occupant. She lay motionless on the floor, arms and legs splayed. Her back was partially leaning against the back wall of the elevator, her neck tilted awkwardly. The diamond on the other ear did not glitter at all; it was barely visible under a coat of blood.

The woman was Natalie. She was surrounded by shards of broken mirror glass, with one large piece protruding from her neck.

Chapter 12

November 5, 1943

Albert was pacing and holding the side of his head. "What should I do? What should I do?"

He was plagued often by chronic headaches, and today he had a doozy. He blamed them on the injury he suffered in World War I. He had served with the first Canadian Division's fifth Battalion in France, enlisting at only 16 after lying about his age. He had suffered bullet and shrapnel wounds to his head, arms, and stomach. Possessing an unblemished record, he had received an honourable discharge. He hadn't wanted to leave the army. It was the first time in his life he had felt accepted, needed. This was a feeling he had never enjoyed, even from his own family. They had dismissed him like a repugnant outcast. Sent him away as far as they could, tucked him away to no longer be a blemish on their good family name. He would never forgive them. He wasn't good enough for them, an embarrassment he once overheard them say. The next thing he knew he was on a ship, leaving his home in England to start a new life on his own in Canada. Then the army discharged him too. He was an undesirable once again. He grimaced as he thought of how his life had gone since then. The only bright spot was Edith.

Why had he promised to take her to Vancouver? It was impossible! He knew why he'd asked her. It was his way of keeping her. He could not bear to lose her, not like Lottie.

The pain in his head increased. He was not a rich man and could not afford any more gifts to entice her to stay with him. The gold watch he had given her was purchased on credit. He knew the watch would only keep her from going to those Saturday night dances for a short time. If she did go, he knew she would meet some handsome young man and then she would leave him. Just like everybody else, she would want to get rid of him.

She was so beautiful. He just couldn't allow her to do it. Finally, he devised a plan. Edith hated winter and he knew it, so one night, when they were sitting in his room, he said, "Why don't we go to Vancouver? The weather is much milder."

Edith's eyes widened. "Vancouver! I've never been. I hear it's the best."

"Would you really like to go with me?"

"I think it would be just wonderful. Do you mean it?"

"If it's what you want, why not?"

"Oh yes! Let's do it!"

"Okay, then. It's settled. We'll go."

His promises and the lies escalated through October and into November. Edith became more excited about the adventure with each passing day. It was all she talked about. Albert enjoyed listening to her plan their departure. He told Edith his wife lived in Vancouver, which was about the only truthful thing he said. We can stay with her, he told her. She'll take good care of you.

They would travel by train, he told her. As soon as they arrived, she could start work. He had already lined up a job for her as a blueprint maker for $125 a month.

With each new lie Edith became more enthralled. It all sounded so wonderful and exciting. She could hardly wait.

As the weeks passed, the weather got colder. She was tired of waiting and just wanted to go. She began to notice that whenever she tried to pin Albert down to a definite departure date, he would suddenly become quiet. When she pressed him for an answer, he would become evasive or make excuses. Edith began to suspect that they were never really going to Vancouver. It was all just a pipe dream, or a lie. She no longer spoke excitedly about their plans, and Albert could see her discontent.

Albert and Edith spent all their free time together, but one evening he couldn't find her. He was beside himself. He went outside and sat on the bench in front of the rooming house. Despite a thin layer of snow on the sidewalk, a young girl was out skipping. Even in her heavy boots and large mittens, she still managed to turn and jump the rope quite well. Albert watched her. When she missed a skip, she folded her rope and came to sit on the bench beside him.

"Why so glum, mister?"

"Who's glum, not me," he said, and forced a smile at her.

"Where's Edith?"

"Don't know."

"I could be your friend."

"Well, that's a very nice offer, but I'm not a very good skipper like you."

"That's okay, I can teach you."

Just then, Edith came out the front door of the boarding house. She saw them on the bench and hoped they had not spotted her. She tried to duck through the fence to make an exit at the back lane.

"Edi-i-i-th," called the young girl.

She had no choice, so she walked toward them.

"Edith," Albert said. "Where have you been? You didn't answer your door."

"Oh, I must have had the radio on too loud."

Albert noticed her hair was done and she had her lipstick on.

"I've got great news," he said. "Come sit down."

The young girl got up and resumed her skipping.

"What?" asked Edith, a tone of suspicion in her voice.

Albert held her hand and leaned towards her to whisper in her ear.

"We leave December fifth."

"We do?"

Forgetting to act grown-up, she jumped up from the bench and clapped her hands with glee.

"There's so much to do."

Albert laughed. He was excited, too. He almost believed it himself. Deep down he knew they could never really go. Despite knowing this, he couldn't help but share her enthusiasm.

It wasn't just the lack of funds. The biggest obstacle was the fact that he was not allowed to leave Winnipeg. It was a condition of his release. Still he hated to disappoint her, and knew in doing so he would lose her.

He had made a concerted effort to make it happen. First, he needed to solve the money issue. He contacted the Canadian Legion for financial assistance, claiming his wife was sick. They unofficially agreed, but the Bank of Commerce declined his loan request. He received a $25 advance from his job as a mechanic, and was able to obtain a $50 loan from a fellow employee. He was beginning to get his hopes up, but they faded when he approached the National Selective Service to ask for a release to travel to Vancouver. They declined his request.

As far as Edith knew, they were to leave in just a few days. Albert gave her the $50 his fellow employee had lent him, and told her to buy herself a nice pair of shoes for travelling. She politely thanked him and tried to mask her excitement at the thought of purchasing new shoes for the trip. He saw the glint in her eye and knew how much it meant to her. It made him both happy and sad at the same time. He stood outside the rooming house on Spence Street and smiled at her as she skipped down the street heading to the shops. He felt a tap on his back, turned, and there was the young girl who lived downstairs. She was holding a skipping rope and looked up at him.

"You want me to teach you how to skip, mister?"

"Not today," he said. He patted her on the head and then he went inside.

When Edith returned with her prized possessions already on her feet, Albert told her what a wonderful choice she had made. How lovely they looked. As she stood pointing one foot out for him to admire, he added how grown up and sophisticated she looked in them. He told her all the things she wanted to hear. Edith was so happy and excited. Until Albert frowned when she told him she'd give up her room at the end of the month and stay a few nights with her parents before they left. He was quiet a moment and she asked, "What's wrong, don't you want me to?"

"Oh no," he said, smiling. "But that would ruin my other big surprise. I have a few nights booked at the Marlborough Hotel before we leave, isn't that much better?"

"At the Marlborough Hotel, oh yes, that would be wonderful!"

On December 2, 1943, Edith arrived at the Marlborough at 7:00 p.m. and was given room #503. She wore a pretty blue dress, her gold watch, and best of all, her new shoes. She couldn't have been happier.

Albert continued pacing in his room, his headache getting worse.

"What should I do? What should I do?"

Then the only logical solution came to mind, and a sense of relief engulfed him.

Chapter 13

May 27, 2013

Bedlam ruled the fifth floor.

Once he discovered Natalie splayed unconscious on the elevator floor in a thickening pool of blood, Steve sprang into action. He jabbed the stop button, and as the alarm screamed he jammed his body against the closing door. There was time for one quick look while he took her pulse. It was weak, but there.

"What are you doing?" Penny was pleading. She couldn't see what was happening in the elevator. All she knew was she felt horrible and weak, and blood from her toe was beginning to seep through the towel.

Steve didn't answer. She heard him call Randall to get an ambulance. "Send them to the elevator's on the fifth floor." Thinking of Penny he added, "Make that two, and find Alec and send him here too, and make it quick!"

He hung up.

Steve's mind worked fast. An accident or foul play? There was no time to think. He tore off his shirt and tied it around Natalie's wound. Shouting her name did nothing. Even so, he spoke comforting words to her on the chance she could hear him.

"It's OK. You're going to be fine. The ambulance is on the way."

"Who are you talking to?" Penny asked.

"Sit tight, Penny."

Hearing the urgency in his voice, she couldn't bear it. She rose from the chair and hobbled to the elevator. One look at the horrific scene and she fainted.

Steve flipped open his cellphone again. It only rang twice.

"Dan Peters, Homicide."

"Dan, it's Steve."

"Hey Steve, how—"

"We have a problem at the Marlborough. We got an injured woman in the elevator, fifth floor, ambulance on the way."

Thinking Natalie may be listening he added, "I'm sure she'll be fine. Just thought you'd want to send someone over to check things out. Pronto!"

"On our way," said Dan and clicked off.

Steve had said pronto and Dan knew what that meant. It was their old code. It meant foul play was suspected, possibly murder. As much as Steve hoped Natalie was going to make it, he had a sinking feeling that she wouldn't.

Some of the other fifth-floor occupants started coming out of their rooms, drawn by the elevator alarm. Some were in housecoats, others in nightgowns, and one man was in his underwear.

Steve glared at them. "Stay back," he commanded.

Randall and Alec burst through the stairwell door at the end of the hallway and ran toward him. They accidentally bumped into the man in his underwear and he yelled at them. They saw Steve, wearing no shirt and blocking the elevator doors. Then they saw Penny lying in a heap, a blood-soaked towel wrapped around her foot. Alec noticed a trail of blood droplets leading from room 503 to the elevator.

Alec's concern turned to rage. He glared up at Steve, waving his fist. "What the—"

Then he saw Natalie and froze.

"Nataleeeeeeeeee..." It was a maniacal yell, scarcely human. He crawled toward her.

The ambulance attendants arrived and Steve waved them into the elevator. Chief Dan arrived with a couple of uniforms.

The ambulance attendants went to work quickly and efficiently, following orders from the man with no shirt. They soon had Natalie on the stretcher and headed to the service elevator down the hall. Alec went with them.

"What about her?" asked the next set of attendants.

"Cut toe, may need stitches," Steve told them. "She drank a fair bit of alcohol today. Fainted a few minutes ago."

Penny had regained consciousness by then, but kept quiet. She gave Steve a dirty look after his comment about the alcohol before she shifted her attention to the attendants who prepared to take her to the hospital.

Randall looked stricken. He stood back, shifting from one foot to the other.

It was then Steve noticed that the two uniforms were the same ones who had been in the hotel the night Carla was stuck in the elevator. They looked shocked to see that Steve was in charge, and even more shocked that Chief Dan was allowing it. They seemed pleased when the Chief finally said to Steve, "Thanks Steve. We'll take it from here."

Steve took this hard, but knew it was the way things were. Still, he sat in the chair watching their every move, wanting to be sure everything was done right, with no shortcuts.

He thought of Penny, and how she had used his cell just a little while ago to call her parents. It seemed a long time ago. He opened his phone, found the number she had dialed, and called them to let them know what had happened.

After that, Steve resumed his watch over the investigation that was still underway. It frustrated him to see that they were taking samples from the blood that had dropped from Penny's toe from his room. That ought to confuse them for a while. When they went into his room, he got up and followed them in. One of the uniforms, the tall one, stood at the door and put out his arm to stop him.

"Hey, come on," Steve said. "It's my room."

"Sorry."

Steve returned grudgingly to sit in the wing chair. They spent a long time in his room and carried out several items in bags. Steve hoped it wasn't anything he needed.

Dan walked over and passed him a cup of hot coffee with cream and one sugar, just the way he liked it. Steve looked up at Dan's face. It was careworn, but kind. He still looked good for his age, always had.

"Looks like you might be almost ready to come back."

"Thanks for the coffee, Chief. As for the job offer, that's pretty generous of you and I'd be a fool to pass it up. Honestly though, I'm just not sure..."

Chief Dan's phone rang and as he fumbled to get it out of his pocket he looked Steve in the eye, "You mull it over and let me know."

When he finished his call he took a deep breath, "Got some bad news," he said. "The lady in the elevator, she didn't even make it to the hospital."

Steve lowered his head, placed his face in both his hands, and was silent.

Dan waited a few moments to allow Steve to absorb this information before he delivered the next blow.

"Steve. I'm going to have to ask you to come in and answer some questions."

"Sure," Steve said. "I understand. Could you grab me a shirt, Chief?"

Chapter 14

During questioning at the station, Steve was beyond co-operative. He was ready to tell them everything he knew. Usually on the other side of the interrogation table, he knew the importance of a compliant witness. He would do whatever he could to assist with the investigation.

He was disappointed to discover that Chief Dan would not be present. Instead, the interrogation had been left to the two new detectives Steve had never met. They both looked pretty young to Steve, but the shorter, callow one in particular. That one is still wet behind the ears, Steve thought to himself. The taller detective was likely pretty young too, but it was his air of confidence made him appear older, more experienced. It was his smugness that really irritated Steve. Before they could get started questioning him, Steve launched in.

"I don't know what happened there tonight, but if it wasn't some freakish accident, it's pretty obvious who's responsible."

"Thanks for that, Steve," said the taller detective, who seemed to be running the show. "But please allow us to go through our questions. Surely you, more than anyone, can understand that."

"Sure, yeah, sorry," he said. "Go ahead."

"What was your relationship with the deceased?"

"You mean Natalie Kent. Nat was a great lady. Classy, demure, yet she stood up for herself when she had too. Quite honestly, I don't feel I knew her all that well. Not sure if anyone really did. But what I knew of her, I liked."

"The deceased—"

"Would you quit calling her that? Her name was Natalie."

The other detective scribbled a note on his pad.

"Sorry...Natalie then. She died, presumably from a neck wound inflicted by a piece of broken mirror. We'll have to wait for the autopsy to confirm. Now, coincidentally or not, we found pieces of broken mirror in the bathtub in your room. Can you tell us how they got there?"

After a brief moment of confusion, the severity of the situation hit Steve hard. They weren't questioning him as a witness. He was a suspect! Before he could formulate a response, the detective hurled another question at him.

"There was also a trail of blood from 503, your room, leading to the elevator. Can you tell us whose blood this was and how it got there?"

Steve was pissed. Here he was, ready to help them out and now they were turning on him. If he was a suspect, these idiots needed some serious help.

"Did you Einsteins not notice the mirror from the elevator wall was broken, and did you even see the young lady with the bleeding toe?"

"I'll ask the questions—maybe we should back up. What can you tell us about pawn shop Jim?"

Holy shit! What does that have to do with anything? These assholes were really treating him as a main suspect. What the hell motive would he have?

"That's it. I'm going to need a lawyer before I say any more," he said.

Steve had lied. He wasn't ready to lawyer up just yet. He just couldn't bear to take part in this ridiculous line of questioning. A waste of time, in his opinion, time that could be better spent trying to figure out what actually happened. These novice detectives didn't have a clue, and he sure as hell wasn't going to dredge up the story of Jim with them. The other detective that had been relegated to note taking looked up at the other detective and rolled his eyes. They exchanged knowing glances and then they both left the room.

....

Left sitting in the stark, grey room alone, Steve remembered the last time he was in there. It was after he had shot and killed Jim Kobac. It had been Chief Dan questioning him that time, and it was nothing like the scene that had just occurred here. Dan was compassionate and understanding. He never suspected Steve for a second. He told Steve right off the bat that he knew it was self-defence. He knew Steve would never take the law in his own hands.

"You're no vigilante, Steve. You've got too much respect for the law," he had said.

Steve hadn't been so sure. If he could only remember the moment when the gun went off then he could be as sure as Chief Dan.

A retrieval of the pawnshop security camera proved his innocence. It clearly showed Jim leaping to attack him and ramming into his gun, causing it to fire. Steve had watched the video many times. It certainly did look like self-defence, or even an accident, but it was the look in his own eyes, and he remembered his thoughts just before it happened. He had wondered who would be the creep's next victim. How much more pain would he cause? Then all he could see was Sidney's face and his mind had gone blank.

....

"I hear you're giving my new recruits a tough time," said Chief Dan, smiling as he strolled into the interrogation room.

Dan's voice jarred Steve from his thoughts. "Sorry, Chief, but I got to say, they're a couple of real idiots."

Dan smiled knowingly, but didn't respond to the comment.

"Listen Steve, I know you had nothing to do with that poor woman's death. You know the circumstances better than anyone, and you're a highly trained and experienced detective. They're just making assumptions based on the evidence they have so far. You have to admit the evidence is quite damaging against you. Once they have all the facts they'll leave you alone and move on to find the truth. So please, cut the guys some slack. Remember what it was like when you were first learning the ropes."

"Sure Dan, but meanwhile the trail cools." Steve slammed his fist on the table and then looked straight into the Chief's eyes.

He spoke slowly. "If it wasn't an accident, if anyone murdered Natalie, it had to be her husband. He had big-time motive and likely opportunity."

Dan absorbed this information a moment. He pulled a chair out from under the table, turned it around, and sat on it backwards. He folded his arms over the back of the chair and began to twiddle his thumbs. Steve could almost hear the cranks turning in his head. He knew Dan's patterns well.

Finally Dan spoke. "Exactly what would the motive be?"

"Motives, plural. First of all, there's money and power. When Alec and Natalie got married, her Dad made sure he signed a pre-nup. Her Dad passed away shortly after the wedding, and Natalie became sole heir to his money plus the hotel. Even though Alec managed the place, she was the owner, the boss with the final word. Take Nat out of the picture and now Alec is owner of the hotel and can run it as he sees fit."

"That's a lot of motive."

"Yeah, and there's more. The staff believes he's having an affair."

"Well, even if we couldn't prove the affair, we've got motive covered. But motive alone isn't enough. We need opportunity. Apparently he has an alibi."

"You've questioned him already?"

"Briefly, and unofficially. Since he had an alibi and because we haven't ruled it out as an accident, we decided not to interrogate him. Not yet anyway."

"Oh, but it was decided to question me?" Steve rolled his eyes.

"What was his alibi, anyway?"

"One of the maids. Claims he was on the second floor helping her move a TV."

"Really," said Steve. "Would her name happen to be Carla?"

"Sure is. How'd you know?"

"Guess I must be a mind reader. Did I mention Alec and Natalie had a disagreement about a half-hour before all this happened?"

"No, did you tell the detectives that?"

"Had they given me half a chance I would have told them anything they wanted to know. They were hell-bent on making me the killer. Can you believe they even questioned me about Jim?"

"God, I'm sorry Steve. I'll have a talk with them."

"Do that."

"Tell me something, Steve. What's your gut reaction to this? Do you believe this was a murder or just a freak accident?"

"I don't know Dan. I'm too close to this one to trust my gut. The evidence will have to tell you that. If it is murder, though, I suspect Alec is your man."

"You know the guy. Is he capable of it?"

"I'd hate to think so, but a lot of folks have been convicted of crimes you would never have thought they were capable of committing."

"That's true enough. Let's call it a night, and thanks for your help, Steve. I'll give you a ride back to the hotel if you like."

"That would be great, thanks."

"And Steve… at the risk of sounding like a broken record, any time you're ready to come back, won't be too soon for me. I could sure use you around here."

After all Steve had been through, since Sidney's murder and pulling the trigger on Jim, to have Chief Dan even make such an offer was overwhelming for him. He had never really imagined he'd ever come back, but the events of this day had him questioning this decision. It was obvious he was needed here, he just wasn't sure he could do it yet. "I can see you could use the help, Chief. I promise I'll give it some serious thought, and thanks, it means a lot to me for you to make the offer."

....

The investigation went on for another month. The lab determined that the mirror glass in Steve's tub was not the same as the piece removed from Natalie's throat. The blood from Room 503 and in the hallway belonged to Penny only. Steve was cleared of all suspicion.

Alec's alibi, supplied by Carla, held up as well. According to Carla, she had called Alec for help moving a TV console after the remote fell behind it. Steve was gone from the bar by then with his burgers, and Natalie had left to check on the banquet.

A lightning storm that caused havoc with the hotel electrical could plausibly have jarred the elevator to a sudden stop. That could explain Natalie's bump at the back of her head and the shattering of the mirror on the wall. As there were no prints on the mirror, it was possible the jolt sent a shard flying fatally into her neck.

As far as they could tell from the security tape footage, Natalie was alone in the elevator. She had entered on the ninth floor by herself. The elevator lights had lit up on the eighth floor but everything was dark, and with the history of the elevator's unscheduled stops it was assumed no one got on or off. There was no footage on the seventh floor, and Randall admitted he may have missed setting that camera. In truth, he had been more intent on watching the comings and goings on the fifth floor, when Steve was carrying Penny to his room.

With no suspects, no one with any known motive, and the fact that the elevators had a history of malfunctioning, it appeared to be just a horrible accident. The investigation was over.

Most of the hotel staff were relieved that a murderer was not lurking among them. Still, some remained unsettled. If not a live murderer, perhaps the resident ghost had caused this calamity. What would happen next? Until now, the ghost had only been an inconvenient prankster. This time she had gone too far. No, the air had not yet cleared. Speculation and fear continued to spread.

Chapter 15

On the surface, it was business as unusual at the Marlborough. Two months had passed since the grisly discovery of Natalie in the elevator. Small talk had reverted to the weather, or lack of it.

Natalie's funeral had long since come and gone. It had been well attended of course, and Alec had hosted a grand event afterwards. He included all her friends and family and any hotel staff not scheduled to work. He even renamed the ballroom: it was to be called 'The Natalie.' In addition, he had commissioned a life-size, oil on canvas of her to grace the room. A nice gesture, Steve thought. Perhaps a bit ostentatious, but it seemed to please her family and friends, so Nat would have approved.

Steve couldn't help but wonder if Alec's motives were genuine or the product of a guilty conscience. He had to admit that Alec had changed since Natalie's death. The man truly appeared to be in mourning. He had lost his edge, didn't give the staff such a hard time, and often would just sit and stare. The hotel was slipping, too. Invoices weren't paid on time, and orders weren't placed so they were often running out of essentials. It turned out Natalie, without anyone realizing it, had done more than her share of work running the hotel. As a result, the morale of the staff had plummeted. Steve felt bad. But, what could he do? He kept the place secure, but beyond that, there wasn't much else he could do to change things.

On a Saturday morning, Steve set foot in the lobby to find it buzzing with the arrival of new guests. With the warmer weather and the many summer festivals, it was peak season for visitors to Manitoba.

When he was younger, Steve used to enjoy attending some of the local festivals. He recalled going with his brother and their buddies, with the main lure being to meet the girls that also attended. Thinking back on those days, he could barely recognize himself as that fun-loving kid, and he missed him.

Setting these thoughts aside, he manoeuvered through the crowd waiting at the front desk and grabbed a newspaper off the counter. Those waiting to register scowled at him, but let it go when they realized he was just grabbing the paper, not jumping the line.

He tried as usual to get Penny's attention, but she was busy and had pretty much been avoiding him since that fateful night. Every time he spoke to her, she blushed and turned away. He couldn't really blame her for ignoring him, but he wished it didn't have to be that way. He was sure she suspected that every time he looked her way, the memory of her sitting naked on the toilet seat invaded his thoughts, and admittedly, she was right. But the scene wasn't worth losing her friendship over, and he wished they could both get past it. He would have liked to erase all the events of that day, especially the latter part. They haunted him day and night.

What he missed most was having lunch with Penny. They had been well on their way to becoming good friends, and he could use a friend like Penny. He seldom warmed up so quickly to someone the way he had with her. Most people he didn't mind, and many he simply endured, but there were very few he felt he could befriend. As he picked up his paper, he noticed Randall was also behind the front desk, which surprised him.

"Hey Randall," he said. "What are you still doing here? Isn't your shift over?"

"Very busy, can't talk," said Randall, without even looking up to acknowledge Steve.

Steve shrugged, folded his paper, tucked it under his arm, and headed to the café for his breakfast. Randall busy, he thought. That's a new one.

....

After the rush of new guests at the front desk cleared, Penny put her hand on Randall's shoulder. "Thanks for staying Randall; I wouldn't have survived without you. Everything is such a mess around here."

"No problem, Penny," said Randall, "I see you're still giving our good man Steve the cold shoulder."

Penny frowned, "No I'm not. I'm just busy."

Randall was still punching a few last entries into the computer and Penny, desperately wanting to change the subject, asked him, "Since when do you know so much about the computer, anyway? You hardly ever use it."

"I'm not just a pretty face, you know," he said, smiling.

Penny rolled her eyes and smiled too. "Well, no one would ever accuse you of that," she said, and added, "You can go now if you want. It's quieted down quite a bit."

"That's OK, no rush."

He pointed to a stack of paper. "Has Alec been around to pay those invoices?"

"No, and I get harassed all day by collectors. I'm running out of excuses."

"Why don't I help out? I used to watch Natalie do it," he said. "We just enter the amounts in the accounting program and write the cheques. Then all we have to do is get Alec to sign 'em."

"I can't believe you, Randall. You're really something. All this time I thought you'd just been sleepwalking around here." She laughed.

"I only do what needs to be done. Why do more than that?"

Penny was relieved to have Randall's help. Her mind had been mush lately, and she couldn't have done half of what he was accomplishing. Ever since that day at the beach, waking up in Steve's room and all the rest of it, she had been a wreck. Her safe, comfortable existence was gone. Instead, she was plagued by upset and confusion. Except for lunches with Steve, nothing had actually changed in her life or her routine, yet it was as if she were living someone else's life.

The hotel seemed to have changed, too. Even Randall was no longer the person she once knew, or thought she knew. It was as if they were in another dimension or realm.

She yearned to talk to Steve, but she was so utterly embarrassed and ashamed about so many things that she couldn't even look at him. She'd run the events through her mind, over and over, cringing at the memory of each one, remembering every torturous detail. She went through it again for the hundredth time. It began with her stupid plan to loosen Steve's tongue with a little wine to satisfy her curiosity about his past. Then, instead she was the one who drank too much and ended up blabbering on and on, telling Steve things she had locked away long ago. She couldn't remember ever telling anyone all the lewd details of her husband's infidelity. She wondered what else she had told Steve that day; some of it was still fuzzy.

That was just the beginning. As if baring her soul to him in a drunken stupor wasn't enough, she had proceeded to become ill. She can vaguely remember throwing up on the side of the road. After that she must have passed out in the car. Poor guy, surely not the day at the beach he had expected.

After that things just got progressively worse. Not knowing where she even lived, Steve really had no other choice but to take her back to his room. Some men may have taken this as an opportunity, not Steve. Always a gentleman he goes out to get her a burger. How was he to know she'd freak out being left alone in that room? He found out quick enough when she proceeded to run down the hall yelling like a crazy woman, claiming there was a ghost in his room. If it weren't so damn sad it might be laughable.

Then there was the incident in his bathroom. This was a big one. How utterly ridiculous she must have looked sitting naked on his toilet. Thinking about it, she was sure it was the most embarrassing moment of her life. Although at the time, she was more concerned with the blood spurting out of her toe than being embarrassed. This one at least she could blame on him. He should have remembered there was a broken mirror in his tub before telling her to go take a shower!

Finally, and the most unforgivable, was the way she acted when Steve found Natalie in the elevator. There was poor Nat, barely hanging onto life, and Steve trying to do the best he could to save her. What did she do? She couldn't mind her own business for one second. Instead of staying put as Steve had plainly told her to, she just had to hobble over to the elevator and see what was going on. She took one look inside and fainted. Big help! As if he didn't already have enough to deal with.

So how could she ever face him again? Well, quite simply, she couldn't. If Randall had any idea what had happened, he wouldn't think of asking her to talk to Steve. As much as she knew she couldn't resume her friendship with Steve, it was killing her. She really needed to talk to him. He was the only one she felt she could talk to about the subject most on her mind—that Natalie's death was not an accident. She suspected Steve probably thought the same. She had so many questions, and Steve was the only one who might have some answers. At least they could hash it out together. She trusted him, too. The whole thing was driving her crazy.

Penny had become obsessed with Natalie's death. Not only did she believe it wasn't an accident, but she was also convinced that Alec had something to do with it. She wondered if Steve thought so, too. If Alec was guilty, she was sure with Steve's help they could prove it.

It wasn't a personal vendetta. She actually didn't mind Alec when she had first started working at the hotel. They got along

OK. It was only when she began to suspect he was cheating on his wife that she had become cool towards him. She showed her reproach by ignoring him as much as possible and keeping any conversations brief. She would not look him in the eye, either. This irritated him, and his counter attack was perpetual teasing and sarcastically referring to her as their bright, shiny Penny. He could see how it bugged her and that amused him. But now Penny really hated him. Cheating on his wife was one thing, murdering her was quite another. If he really did it, she would not allow him to get away with it.

Penny was also obsessed by another murder at the hotel, one that had happened long ago. She had been extremely upset the night she woke up in Steve's room. She had also been very scared. In all the years she had worked at the Marlborough, she had avoided ever leaving the main floor. She had never taken the elevator, had never even seen the much-touted ballroom, all because she was afraid of the ghosts. She had read enough about ghosts and, real or not, she wasn't taking any chances of ever running into one. The lobby had always felt safe, and she had never had any desire to venture any farther in the hotel. She likely never would have, not on her own volition anyway. Then she has to wake up in that room, of all rooms.

It had been dark in the room when something had woken her. Her head had hurt and she felt sick to her stomach. At first, she thought she might be at home in her own bed, but it didn't feel right. Then there had been a flash of lightning that had lit up the whole room, and in an instant she knew exactly where she was. It was Steve's room. She had seen his security guard shirt hanging on a hook. It was the room where Edith had been strangled to death. The thunder roared and the radio had come on by itself. That was when she screamed and bolted.

She was incredulous that Steve had left her there alone. If she hadn't been so scared she would have been furious. It still made her shiver just to think about it.

Besides scaring her half to death, something had happened while she was in that room. It had piqued a deep curiosity and sadness with the events surrounding Edith's murder. It also made her feel very unsettled; she felt there was unfinished business. There was something that needed to be done. She just couldn't put her finger on what it was. It seemed just out of reach. She yearned to talk to Steve about that too, but how could she? Not after everything that had happened.

Worst of all she could no longer seek refuge in her beloved books. She hadn't been able to read since that fateful night. She had tried, many times. When she got home from the hospital and had to rest her toe a few days, her Mom had picked up a fresh supply of her favorite authors from the library. When she opened the books she found it impossible to concentrate. Her mind wandered and a paragraph she thought she had just read was gone, with no recollection of what it was about. This, her only comfort and solace, had been taken from her. When her mind wasn't buzzing, working overtime, she would sometimes find herself crying, for no apparent reason. It was like someone had popped the cork on the bottle of her emotions.

The front desk bell sounded. Assuming it was a guest arriving, Penny snapped out of her daydream.

It sounded again. Randall was hitting the bell, smiling, trying to get her attention. Penny realized Randall was doing all the work, and his shift was over.

"Sorry," she said, smiling apologetically. "Do you need me to do anything?"

"Not really, but could you go to the café and get us a couple of coffee and cinnamon buns? And ask them if they need any supplies. I'm going to put in an order."

"You are?"

"Sure, it can't be that hard."

Penny hesitated, remembering that Steve had likely been headed to the café.

"Oh go on, he won't bite you."

She grabbed a newspaper for herself for security, in case she had to wait. At least she could feign engrossment in the headlines and keep to herself. She headed reluctantly to the café.

The café was busy. Steve was sitting by the far window. He either hadn't noticed her come in or was pretending he hadn't. Busy as they were, the young server came to warm up his coffee and gave him a big smile. Penny noticed he diverted his attention from his paper and said thank you. He said something else, too, that she couldn't make out, and then gave the server a silly grin. The server giggled and walked away happy. He was wearing his firmly pressed security uniform and Penny assumed the young server found him quite handsome.

It was while she was frowning at this exchange that Steve noticed her. To her surprise, he only winked at her and then went back to reading his paper. What a jerk, Penny thought. She whisked by him to the kitchen. She proceeded to pour two cups of coffee and put two cinnamon buns on a plate. She told the closest server that she was putting in an order for supplies and asked if they needed anything. She wasn't trying to take credit for putting in the order when Randall was actually doing it; it was just that there was no reason for any explanation.

"Have to get back to you later, too busy right now," was the reply.

She shrugged and continued on her way. There was no way out but to pass by Steve's table. To make matters worse, she had to walk slowly to balance the two coffees plus the cinnamon buns.

"Got a date?" asked Steve.

"Hardly," she said. "Randall's helping me out, so I'm keeping him fed and full of caffeine."

There. She had spoken to him.

"He's still here?"

"Yeah, I know. It's kind of creepy that he's paying invoices and putting in orders. He's actually a whiz on the computer."

"Who'd have thought," said Steve.

The brief conversation had come about naturally, but Penny was now getting flustered. Realizing this, Steve resumed reading his paper and Penny shuffled off, almost tipping over one of the coffees.

At least she spoke to me, thought Steve, and smiled to himself.

Chapter 16

Like a bad storm, a death is prone to manifest strange and unexpected changes in those caught in its wake. Steve knew this; he had seen it happen many times. Some might attribute the changes to a state of mourning, but Steve believed there was more to it than that.

The police claimed Natalie was alone in the elevator, but the more common belief was that she wasn't. A spirit presence was long suspected to ride up and down the elevator shaft. What was once just hotel folklore now carried reverberations of foreboding, fear and angst. Many were convinced Natalie's death was no accident. They blamed it on the ghost of Edith. Once just an innocent prankster, she had now escalated to an evil presence, not one to be toyed with or angered. A presence to be avoided at all costs. This was true for even those who had previously laughed at the ghost stories. They had teased the staff that claimed to have seen or sensed her presence. Now they were silent on the subject, and those who had long believed that Edith was responsible for the malfunctions of the elevator nodded knowingly. The staff took the stairs now, and when they couldn't avoid the elevator, they made sure they never rode it alone. They could often be seen looking nervously over their shoulders at the slightest sound, real or imagined.

Steve was a skeptic, but he had to admit there were things that went on that made even him wonder. On the surface he presented an amused indifference. No sense adding credence to the frenzy of suspicions. He would laugh to himself about how many unsolved cases he could have closed by blaming ghosts. Tough to prove and prosecute, and how on earth would you keep them locked up? He chose not to share this humour, as he knew it would only serve to aggravate and cause hurt feelings. He supposed they needed this explanation to deal with it, and he allowed them to it.

Then there was Randall. The change in him since Natalie's death was the most noticeable. The sleepy night clerk was now practically running the place. Steve supposed it was Randall's own way of dealing with the tragedy.

Steve missed the old Randall, his lazy, relaxed ways and the multitude of jokes and pokes. The new Randall was too busy for his own tomfoolery. Steve hoped it would eventually subside, and almost craved one of Randall's bogus attempts to spark romance in Steve's monkish existence. He could wait it out though, and decided to enjoy the reprieve.

It was the changes in Penny that caused Steve the most concern. She'd hardly said boo to him in a month. He was okay with that, but hoped she'd eventually come around and they could resume their friendship. He hadn't seen her open a book since Natalie's death. After the revealing trip to the beach, he had come to realize her books were her escape. After all she'd told him about her failed relationships he suspected the books she read offered a safe respite. Steve wanted her to be safe.

Alec? Now there was a real puzzle. At one moment, Steve was sure Natalie's death had not been an accident, and wondered if Alec had effectively carried out the perfect murder. Yet, at other times, he felt compassion and sympathy for Alec. It was obvious Alec was lost without Natalie. He could barely run the hotel. Steve tried to spend more time with him, not sure, if it was out of kindness, or curiosity. They often lunched together at the bar now that Penny took her lunch break outside the hotel. At one of these lunches with Alec, Steve was surprised when Carla arrived at their table and insisted she had to speak with Alec right away, and privately.

"Not now, Carla. Can't you see Steve and I are busy?"

"Busy? You're having lunch!" she said.

"I said we're busy and I'll talk with you later."

Carla remained standing at their table, pouting insistently.

"We have some security issues to discuss. I'll talk to you when we're done."

Steve was more than surprised that Alec was even humouring her, let alone making up excuses. Moreover, he was lying. They were just having lunch, as far as he knew.

"Fine." Carla walked away at a fast pace, hips swinging as seductively as ever.

"Lover's spat?" ventured Steve.

Alec gave him a long grave look, but said nothing. Instead, he read the menu he knew by heart.

Steve looked blankly at his own menu and reflected on how things had changed so much around the hotel. He hadn't been here that long, and despite his tendency for detachment, he was starting to feel part of it. Now it had all changed, it was as if everyone else had become remote. His career in homicide had taught him the importance of keeping a professional distance, yet he found the loss of Natalie hard to accept. All his emotions were heightened. Even his sleep had become restless. He dreamt constantly about the young girl. It was as if she were trying to tell him something, but it was always just out of his reach. And there was something new. The girl now had blinding bright, diamond earrings. In a strange way it made sense. The two were becoming one in his dreams. He would wake from these dreams soaked in sweat, heart beating fast, yet he had no idea why. It was as if they both needed something from him, but he could not understand.

In the light of day he would try to rationalize these haunting nightmares. What did they mean, or did they mean anything? It wasn't like him to worry about nightmares. He would normally just wake up and forget about them. These were different; they haunted him. All his efforts to dismiss them were futile. He rationalized it probably had a lot to do with his preoccupation with Natalie's death. The case was closed, but he still had questions. Was it an accident or was it murder?

In the old days, his best friend for closing a case was evidence. He relied on it; his close attention to detail and his thoroughness usually guaranteed success. He had to face the fact: he was a security officer at the Marlborough, not a detective. He half wondered if he should go back now, just for Natalie. It would give him access to evidence. He knew he could solve this one way or another. He was sure those novice detectives had just taken the easy route and labelled Natalie's death accidental, case closed. He needed to do something, but just when he thought he might be able to go back, he would remember Jim. He had truly hated Jim, hated all Jim stood for. He was even glad Jim was dead. It was why he wasn't ready to go back. How could he? He who claimed to value life so highly, how could he be glad the man was dead?

He thought back to the chilling moment when Jim's mother had been notified of his death. She had been destroyed; he was her only son, gone. A mother can easily ignore the misdeeds of the man by remembering the boy. It had broken her heart, and he understood why she had glared at him with hate in her teary eyes.

At the time, Chief Dan had insisted Steve talk to someone. Someone was, of course, a shrink—Phil Cleaver, an employee of the department, who had heard enough a long time ago. Steve went, knowing it was standard procedure. He went to the weekly sessions and told Phil everything the man wanted to hear. He never let out his true feelings—his relief that Jim was dead, off the streets and the disgust he felt for himself because of it. How he couldn't convince himself it was self-defence, how he felt responsible for not being able to get Sidney off the streets. Instead he told him all the right things. In less than two months, Phil cleared him to return to duty. Chief Dan was relieved, until Steve handed in his resignation. Dan tried to convince him otherwise and the two men compromised: Steve would be on a leave of absence for an undetermined duration.

After that, Steve retreated to his apartment, living on his savings, rarely going out. He had felt the need for self-punishment; he was depressed, he knew that. He ate, but barely, and he drank. He drank—a lot, and alone.

....

Eventually Steve had enough. He woke up one morning and decided it was time for a change. It was a sunny day and he decided to get out, even just for a moment or two. Instead of his usual sweatpants, he grabbed his jeans out of the drawer and was astounded when he put them on. They were much too big. He examined himself in the full-length mirror. His cheeks were sunken and deep wrinkles had formed around his tired eyes. He turned to look around his apartment. It was a godawful mess. He sniffed and the odour of stale booze and filth filled his nostrils. He had never been a heavy drinker, and although the booze numbed the pain, he was beginning to realize it had just made matters worse.

He left the apartment, and once out on the street he began to walk, and then the walk turned into a run. He ran for a long time. When he returned, he slept. He did the same thing the next day, but after his run, he stopped and picked up a burger. When he arrived back at the apartment the smells and the mess made him lose his appetite, so he began to clean. He threw out his empties and even a bottle of whiskey that was still half-full. He scrubbed and cleaned until the place shone. Even the cloudy windows sparkled, allowing him to see out of them clearly. He noticed a large tree whose branches swayed gently in the wind. He admired its beauty, envied its freedom. Then he ate his burger, cold. Every day he ran and he even began to eat regularly. Healthy food replaced the junk food. He became strong, and slowly his deep depression began to lift.

Throughout his drinking and depression, he hadn't noticed how quickly his savings had dwindled and how his credit cards had nearly maxed out. He knew it was time to get a job. One morning, after his run, he picked up a paper on his way to breakfast. Sipping a coffee, he flipped to the Help Wanted section. There were several listings, but none interested him. He noticed a job listed for a security guard at a hotel. He reviewed it dubiously and moved on. After looking over the other opportunities, he realized the security job was really the only one that suited his abilities and experience. It was a huge step down from homicide detective, but he needed a job. The more he considered it, the more he warmed up to it. No real pressures, no one he knew, a fresh start. There was also the opportunity to rent a furnished room on a monthly basis.

So here he was, a security guard trying to pretend he was still a detective. After the night of Natalie's death and the subsequent interrogation he endured, he had tried to let it go. He tried to mind his own business. It was no use. He couldn't help it. He craved the comfort of the truth for closure and peace of mind. He wondered how much was driven by his quest for justice or his innate need to find the answers, put it all together neatly, and put it to rest. He did know a big part of it was his need to protect. If there were a killer among them, who was to say, he wouldn't kill again. He also felt a strong urge to find out for Natalie. Not that she cared now, but her memory deserved the truth, whatever it was.

Steve would go over the events of that evening, over and over again. He started to put the sequence of events down on paper, and taped the sheets in order on the wall of his room. He was sure he had all the facts straight, but continued to have a nagging feeling that he was missing something. It haunted him. Hard as he tried, he could not figure it out what it was. What had he overlooked? It festered in his mind until his head ached. He knew it had to be an important fact to bother him so much. He just could not remember. The only clue he could retrieve was that it had to do with the elevator. But what?

Penny might help, he considered, but she would barely speak to him.

What was it? He knew that whatever it was, it could help him solve the puzzle, once and for all.

Chapter 17

It was now nearing the end of July and so far, it had not been the summer weather normally expected. After months of below-normal temperatures, everyone had expected July to be the usual month of sizzling heat. There had been a few warm days, but none so hot.

Nevertheless, it was not the weather that occupied Penny's thoughts at the front desk that morning. She had become obsessed with Natalie's death. She did not believe it was an accident; she could feel it in her bones. She had a strong desire to share her thoughts with Steve. She just couldn't, though. She could barely face him, let alone have a conversation. It was driving her crazy. She was so distraught and preoccupied that even her books could not offer her comfort. Her concentration was elsewhere, surprisingly in the real world. She had to do something.

She scoured the Internet searching for information. She searched under murder, how to solve a murder, archived news, police files—anything that would help. This was her focus at work now, diverted only by the interruption of guests. Almost every new arrival coming to the front desk said the same thing, or a similar variation. "Is summer ever going to get here?" or, "Another rotten day out there again." Penny would smile and mechanically agree, as if it were the first time she had heard it that day. Once they were safely inside, she quickly went back to the computer.

And there it was. It was a news story from the local paper, dated 1943.

WORDLESS WESTGATE SPEAKS NO MORE

By Jim Smithers
Staff writer, Winnipeg Tribune

Albert Victor Westgate was hung by the neck at Headingley Gaol on July 24, 1944, for the murder of Grace (Edith) Cook. He strangled her to death in room 503 of the Marlborough Hotel on December 4, 1943. Edith worked as a waitress at Rae and Jerry's Restaurant in Brathwaites Store at 431 Portage Ave.

Witnesses reported that Westgate entered the hotel a short time after Edith arrived on December 3, 1943. He visited her in room 503.

They were seen together by the front desk clerk, two bellboys, and a chambermaid, all at different times. One chambermaid said that Edith had on a pretty blue dress and new shoes.

Anne Benson, a waitress at a local coffee shop, told reporters she had later seen Westgate at about 5 a.m. on December 5, sitting alone, mumbling repeatedly, "I shouldn't have done it. I shouldn't have done it."

A peculiar event sealed Mr. Westgate's arrest when he returned Edith's new shoes, which he had given her money to buy, to the shoe store, using Edith's original bill of sale.

Mr. and Mrs. John Cook, Edith's parents, revealed that Mr. Westgate had promised Edith he would take her to Vancouver, and told her he had secured a job for her. As it turned out, he had neither the means, nor the liberty, as his previous record would not allow him to leave the province. When he realized the hopelessness of his false promises, they said Westgate chose the course of murder.

They became suspicious when Edith did not come home to say goodbye before taking her trip to Vancouver. They contacted Mr. Westgate, who professed to know nothing.

At about 4:30 p.m. on Sunday, December 5, the Cooks and Westgate went to room 503 at the Marlborough and knocked on the door. There was no answer at the door, but there was a strange smell coming from inside, so they summoned a chambermaid to open the door. Once inside they saw Edith lying in bed with the covers up around her head.

Prior to the murder of Grace Edith Cook, Westgate was convicted of the murder of Charlotte (Lottie) Adams on November 16, 1928, and was sentenced to hang by the neck on January 23, 1929, at the Provincial Gaol. During the trial, Westgate was represented by a lawyer whose services had been engaged by Westgate's prominent and wealthy family in England.

After the sentencing, there was an appeal on the grounds that one of the jurors was suffering from dementia. The new trial, in March 1929, resulted again in a conviction of murder, and execution was scheduled for June 5, 1929. However, on June 3, the Minister of Justice commuted Westgate's sentence to life in prison after receiving a petition circulated by the War Veterans of Manitoba asking for clemency for Westgate, who was a veteran of the First World War.

With help from the War Veterans and due to good behaviour, Westgate served only 14 years of his life sentence and was released on parole on June 3, 1943. He secured a position with Gillis and Warren, where he was employed as a mechanic. Because of his lack of small talk, his co-workers dubbed him Wordless Westgate.

It was in August, following his release from prison, that he met 16-year-old Grace (Edith) Cook. Edith was laid to rest in Brookside Cemetery.

Albert Westgate was born in Kent, England, in 1901. Mr. Westgate was a Remittance Man who has lived in Winnipeg since he was 16. He served in the Canadian Expeditionary Force and the 1st Canadian Divisions' 5th Battalion in France during the First World War.

Although the Criminal Code states that condemned criminals must be buried within the walls of the institution in which they were hung, the War Veterans again came to the aid of Westgate and were granted permission by the Minister of Justice to bury his body in the Military section of Brookside Cemetery. He was buried on July 25, 1944.

Penny read it quickly, and then she took her time. As absorbed as she was, Penny jumped when the lobby elevator dinged. Glancing in its direction, she noticed that nobody exited. Then she felt a cool breeze pass by her and she shivered as some papers on her desk flew off and flittered to the floor.

These events should have catapulted Penny into a tailspin of fright, but instead a tear rolled down her freckled cheek. She picked up the papers and went back to the article. When she came to the part about Edith's parents looking for her, more tears flowed.

There was also a picture of the murderer, Albert Victor Westgate, or Wordless Westgate, as he was known. Penny was shocked to read that he had murdered before. She shuddered at his photo and his vacant eyes that peered back at her from the computer screen. A cold chill ran through her whole body.

As Penny sat behind the counter, her fingers closed around the printout of Wordless Westgate in her pocket. The story had released her from her obsession with Natalie's death, but only for a moment. She knew then that she would have to show it to Steve.

She couldn't stand the fact that everyone blamed Edith for Natalie's death. Now, more than ever, she had to prove who the real murderer was.

Chapter 18

S teve sat on a step in an alley outside the east exit of the hotel. He had been craving some fresh air and some time alone. The sun had come out and shone brightly at one end of the alley. Where he sat it was dark, shaded by a neighbouring building. The air was damp and humid from a recent downpour.

At the end of the alley, he noticed steam rising from what looked like a discarded or lost item of clothing that lay on the ground. The fresh air he had hoped for was tainted with the stale stench from an adjacent garbage bin. It was not the most pleasant spot, but at least it was quiet.

Looking up he saw a fire escape attached to the building across the lane. He immediately thought of Sidney. She had never really had a chance at life. He wished she had let him help her. He should have tried harder, insisted. He blamed himself a little, but knew enough about the streets that the chances of her accepting his offer of help were practically nil, no matter what he did.

He sat quietly and remembered Sidney, not the Sidney that was gone, but the one that was full of life. He smiled, thinking of her spirit, her grit. Deciding to go back in, Steve stretched his long legs to propel him upright on the staircase. As he did so he heard the beep of his phone. He opened the phone and put it to his ear, "Steve Ascot, security." He waited, but there was no reply.

He tried again. "Security, hello, anyone there?" Again, no reply.

Just as he was about to hang it up he thought he should look at the call display to see who it was. The display read, "Meet me in bar @ 12 Pen."

Steve was confused until he realized he had received one of those horrible text messages, his first and hopefully his last. He wasn't too keen on this type of communication. Too one-sided. He had no idea how to reply. No computer geek, he had always relied on the office staff at the station to do his research when he needed it. Then it hit him: it was Penny. He couldn't believe it, even wondered if it was one of Randall's tricks. Either way, it was almost noon and he wasn't going to miss finding out.

He took one last look at the fire escape at the end of the alley and envisioned the horror Sidney must have experienced, falling to her death. Dismissing the thought, he wiped his brow and left to attend to the present. He went back into the hotel and headed straight to the bar.

Not wanting to be late and risk her leaving, if in fact she was there at all, he practically ran down the hallway. He slowed down only at the entrance to the bar and sauntered in, trying to appear relaxed and nonchalant. He was neither. He surveyed the bar and spotted her quickly, sitting at their old table. He took a deep breath and walked over.

Penny didn't notice him until he was standing right there. She looked up, startled to see him looming above her.

"You came," she said.

"I'm sure you expected I would."

He sat down across from her and tasted the beer she had already ordered for him. She sipped her water and avoided looking at him.

"Not having a drink today?" he teased, and then regretted it.

She looked embarrassed. "Nope," was all she said.

After an uncomfortable silence, she began to talk.

"Listen, I'm not a drinker, never have been. And I'm really sorry about that day in Gimli."

"I'm the last person you have to apologize to for that," he said, sheepishly.

"No, let me."

Steve looked as if he was about to say something, but she held up her finger to stop him.

"I'm sorry I was such an idiot, getting drunk, throwing up, leaving you no choice but to take care of me."

"It's all right. I've seen worse."

"You have?"

"What I mean is you have nothing to be sorry about. It's OK."

"Nothing to be sorry about—are you kidding?"

"OK. Apology accepted, let's just forget about it."

"Forget about it, I wish I could. I wish I could forget it all. There's so much more. Then running down the hallway like a madwoman, when you left me alone in that room, which wasn't very nice by the way."

He was relieved to see her temper beginning to flare, the old Penny surfacing.

"How could you leave me alone in there? I have no idea how you can sleep in there at night."

"I was hungry, you were sleeping, so I went out for a burger."

"And then you offer me your shower with a tub full of broken glass. I almost lost my toe, you know."

"This has got to be loveliest apology I've ever received."

"Oh stuff it, let me finish. Worst of all I fainted when you needed me most. Big help, wasn't I?"

"Come on, Pen, I'm almost glad you fainted. You didn't need to see that."

"It was just so horrible, I was horrible. I wish that day had never happened."

"I know. It's OK, Pen. I can handle it, but you know I never get used to it."

Steve reached out and put his hand on top of hers. Penny didn't move her hand away immediately, but she didn't hesitate long either. She pulled it away and reached for the piece of paper she had been reading.

"So, we're good?" she asked.

"We're good."

Penny carefully unfolded the paper. "This is what I really wanted to talk to you about."

She turned the sheet around so it was facing right side up for Steve to read. She leaned toward him, watching his face. After what seemed forever, Steve finally finished reading.

"Where on earth did you get this?"

"Internet."

"The Winnipeg Police files are on the Internet now?"

"Oh no, this is such an old file, historic really, but it was strange. I don't know how I got to it. It just kind of showed up on the screen."

"I don't know how you found it, but it sure is some story. Murder is bad enough, but when a murderer is set free to murder again, that's unforgivable. That's why my old job was so important to me."

Penny thought this may be the perfect opportunity to ask him why he left his job, but decided against it.

"She wants her shoes."

"What?"

"Edith wants her shoes back. That's why she haunts the hotel."

"Oh come on, Penny, you can't believe all that crap."

"I can so. Edith's soul will not rest until she gets her shoes back. I know it."

"Have you ever seen a ghost, Penny?"

"No."

"Well then, what makes you think they exist?"

"Do you only believe in what you can see? There are lots of things in this world that you just can't explain."

"I'll give you that, but ghosts? Come on!"

"Let's go to your room," she said.

"What!" Taken aback at first, he quickly recovered and smiled, "I'm not that kind of guy."

"I bet you are, but give me a break. I want to see if I can sense Edith in the room. I'm sure I did the night I was in there alone."

"Won't you be too scared?" Steve teased.

"Probably, but if you're there I think I'll be OK."

As they were about to leave, the server set down the two orders of fish and chips that Penny had forgotten she had ordered.

"Can we eat first? I'm kind of hungry," Steve said.

He had already started, so she nodded in agreement. She watched as he methodically poked his fork into the fish at one-inch intervals. He reached for the vinegar and sprinkled it carefully into each puncture. He even appeared to be counting and regulating the number of droplets released.

Penny watched his performance. "You got problems, don't you, Steve."

"I just like things done a certain way. You have a problem with that?"

"Not at all. It's almost entertaining."

Steve picked up one of the longer crinkle-cut fries and held it in the air. He waved it around as he spoke.

"There's been something I've wanted to talk to you about, Penny."

Penny had noticed before that Steve often talked with his hands. Now he was talking with a french fry in his hand and he looked utterly ridiculous. She tried to concentrate on his words, but was mesmerized by the dancing fry.

"Quit doing that," she said, pointing at the french fry.

Steve smiled, popped the fry in his mouth, and chewed a moment. He took in a deep breath, filling his nostrils with the smell of stale beer, salt and vinegar.

"There's something I missed the night Natalie died."

"What do you mean?"

"It's hard to explain. When you've been a detective as long as I have, you can sense when you've missed, or overlooked something, even if you can't quite figure out what it is. It's usually pretty important, which is why it drives you crazy. I'm hoping you'll be able to help me remember."

Penny nodded. "It's like when you can't remember a famous person's name, or the name of a song, right?"

"Sort of, only more intense."

"Why do you think I could help? I was barely conscious most of the time."

"You never know."

"You don't believe Natalie's death was an accident either, do you?"

"I'm not sure, but maybe not, no."

"I know who did it," she announced proudly.

"Alec," Steve said.

"Yes!"

"No. I mean, there's Alec. He's waving at us."

Chapter 19

December 1943

Edith stood on the sidewalk outside her rooming house on Spence Street, with all her worldly belongings carefully packed. She was eager to get going, and wished the cab would hurry. It was the beginning of December and the weather had turned cold.

Impatient, yet tired of standing, she decided to sit down on the larger suitcase. Elbows on her knees, she looked down at her feet and smiled with pride. She had never had such a beautiful new pair of shoes. She frowned at a small spot on the toe of the left shoe. She licked her finger and quickly rubbed it off.

When the cab ever arrived, it would take her to meet Albert for coffee. After that, they were going back to her room at the Marlborough. Soon after that, they would be boarding the train to Vancouver. She couldn't believe her luck at meeting Albert; he had been so good to her.

She fidgeted, getting more and more tired of waiting. Finally, she saw the cab making its way down the street toward her. A nice young man who was driving the cab loaded her luggage in the trunk, held the door for her and smiled.

"Going on a trip?" he asked.

"Yes, moving actually. To Vancouver."

"I hear they have great weather. Like to go there myself someday."

"Oh you should," she said. "I'm going by train."

"I bet you'll be the prettiest girl on the train," he said. "Going alone, are you?"

"No, with a friend."

"Too bad."

Neither spoke for the rest of the ride. Edith was consumed with her own thoughts, and the driver had turned up the radio and whistled along to the tunes being played.

Edith thought how she was both excited and nervous about her move to Vancouver. It all sounded so good, almost too good to be true. No more cold Manitoba winters, and she could certainly put up with a little rain. Better than freezing to death. The job Albert had arranged sounded very important. A blueprint maker. She didn't know exactly what a blueprint was. How she would ever make one was a mystery. Nevertheless, she was sure she would learn—at $125 a month, she would be certain to learn. Albert promised she could live with him and his wife, and this worried her. What if his wife didn't like her? What if she didn't like his wife? Well, I won't worry about that, she decided. With my salary, I'll be able to afford a room if it doesn't work out.

As exciting as it all was, she had some regrets, mainly leaving her mom. Her mom worried about her so much, and even though she would be just fine, she knew her mother would be worried sick. She would also miss her job and friends at Rae & Jerry's. She had promised she would write them all often. Some had tried to convince her not to go, but gave up when they realized how determined she was. It was even going to be hard to leave her Dad. He had been dead set against her going, but couldn't hide his approval when she had told him about the job. He had looked impressed.

"Here we are, Miss," said the driver.

Albert was waiting for her in front of the hotel. As soon as the cab pulled up he smiled and waved. Edith thought he looked nervous. The driver quickly walked around to open the door for Edith. Before he could, Albert reached for the door handle.

"I've got it. Just get her bags for her."

Edith saw the driver roll his eyes behind Albert's back, and then he winked at Edith. She tried to stifle a giggle, and Albert noticed and frowned at her.

Albert paid the driver. As they were walking away the driver called, "Have a safe trip and good luck in Vancouver."

"Thank you, bye," said Edith and waved to him.

Albert picked up the larger suitcase with one hand and pulled at her hand with the other.

"You shouldn't be telling strangers your business."

"I'm sorry, I'm just so excited."

Albert squeezed her hand. "You look wonderful Edith. If I didn't know you, I would think you were a real grown-up sophisticated woman."

"And on her way to Vancouver, no less," said Edith, smiling.

Albert squeezed her hand a bit tighter.

Edith looked up at him with adoring eyes, and then rested her head of bouncy auburn curls against his arm.

A quick cup of coffee and then back to her room, thought Albert, as they entered the hotel. He stared straight ahead, his surroundings a blur. His eyes were vacant, as if his soul had momentarily taken leave of his body.

Chapter 20

After that first awkward lunch, Steve and Penny had slipped back into their old habit of lunching in the bar together. They had never made it back to his room for the ghost hunt Penny had hoped for. She was busy at work, and eventually either forgot about it or chickened out. Steve never mentioned it again, on purpose. He thought it was a stupid idea. There were more important things to worry about than imaginary ghosts.

Their lunches together were different now, not as carefree as they used to be. They used the time together to discuss the case, as Penny called it. Their conversations were now all about Natalie's death. Was it an accident or not? They rehashed the details of that night, over and over again. At times, and without much luck, Penny would try to shift the conversation to Edith. She was dismayed that once the police announced it was an accident, the hotel staff had begun to believe that Edith caused the elevator to jolt, which led to Natalie's death. Everyone had long blamed Edith's ghost for the haunting of the hotel, in particular the elevator pranks, so it all fit. This tormented Penny. Edith had suffered enough in her short life. Penny couldn't stand to have the girl's memory tarnished by such fallacy.

It was now nearing the end of August, and Steve was waiting impatiently for Penny to show up. He sat at their usual spot in the bar and kept watching the doorway for her. He had lots to go over with her. He had even written a few points on a napkin, so he wouldn't forget. Penny finally arrived and took a seat opposite him.

"Sorry. I had a new arrival to check in."

"That's OK."

He looked at the napkin and was just about to begin.

Penny leaned over the table and whispered, "We mustn't let him know we suspect him."

"Who?"

"Alec, of course. We're in agreement he did it, right?"

"If you say so, Sherlock."

"If he knows we suspect him he'll start being more careful, erase his tracks."

"I'm sure he has no idea. Those icy stares you give him every time he walks by likely wouldn't tip him off."

"I don't give him icy stares. And besides, if I did, it wouldn't mean anything. I've always looked at him like that."

"OK, OK. But tell me what makes you so certain Alec had something to do with Natalie's death."

"I don't know. I just know he did it."

"Well a woman's intuition is a powerful tool, but let's review the facts. First of all, motive. What was his motive?"

"Easy. He was having an affair with Carla. He knew he'd eventually be found out. And...Natalie wanted Carla fired. Nat owned the hotel too, and he signed a prenuptial agreement before they got married."

"All true. Powerful motives, money, love or lust, whatever it was. And Alec loves this hotel." said Steve.

"Good! So we have motive, and he's the only one I know of who did have a motive."

"True, but I'm not convinced. Do we know for a fact that he was having an affair with Carla? What proof do we have?"

"You don't see how she looks at him!"

"Yeah, that'll stand up in court," he said. "And besides, he told me he wasn't."

"Of course he's going to deny it. They all do."

"First rule of being a detective Pen: don't let it get personal."

Penny blushed, and then scrunched her eyes and stuck her tongue out at him.

"Well that's mature."

"Let's move on."

The server arrived with two clubhouse sandwiches that Steve had already ordered. She smiled at Steve as she put his plate down. He took a large bite, chewed quickly, gulped, and said while pointing a finger sideways, "OK, let's just assume we have the motive. What about opportunity? Alec does have an alibi."

"Duh! An alibi from Carla? How convenient is that?"

"Still, unless we find a way to prove it wrong, Carla's alibi stands."

Penny took a bite out of her sandwich. She thought about the alibi, but drew a blank.

"You're the hot shot detective, why can't you figure it out?" she snapped.

She regretted it before she had even finished saying it. Steve's face tightened, and his eyes squinted. She had hit a sore spot.

"Sorry" she said, and smiled weakly.

"It's OK, you're right. My specialty is, was, evidence, attention to detail. That's what works for me. I don't have access to any of that now."

"Well you would if you'd go back to your real job!"

Steve was quiet for a moment, staring at his plate.

"I can't, Pen."

"You know you can just tell me to shut up once in a while. Tell me to mind my own business."

"You speak your mind. I like that in a person."

"Well, I'm glad you think it's a plus."

Steve shook his head as though it might help extract a lost thought. "If I could only remember what I missed."

"Not that again. Are you sure, you really did? Maybe you're just desperate for a clue"

"I'm sure, trust me on this one. It's the missing link. I know it."

"We'll just have to just go over it step by step. That's how I find things I've misplaced."

"Good idea. I do know it was when I found Nat in the elevator."

"I'm not much help there. I fainted, remember?"

"Not right away. There was a brief moment."

"All I can remember was seeing Natalie lying there, the blood... oh, and a bright light. Then everything went black."

Steve smiled. "A bright light, eh! You just cut your toe, honey. You weren't having a near-death experience."

"Do you want my help or what?"

"Sorry. Go on."

"It wasn't a light, like from a lamp. It was a blinding light. It pierced my eyes so I couldn't see, and then I fainted."

"Interesting, Pen. I noticed her one diamond earring sparkling, but that couldn't be it. Maybe it was the broken mirror on the floor, reflecting the light from the hallway."

"Maybe, but I don't think it was."

Steve glanced at Penny's plate. She had done the great disappearing act again. He didn't know how she could polish off a meal so quickly without him even noticing she was eating.

Penny looked at her watch. "I have to go."

Steve looked at his watch and couldn't believe lunch had gone by so fast. He looked at his list on the napkin and sighed, and then folded the napkin and placed it in his pocket. He took a large bite of his clubhouse and chewed slowly as he watched her walk away. She was wearing her front desk uniform—a light grey skirt and a short-sleeved white blouse. The blouse always looked and smelled freshly laundered, but Steve longed to run an iron over it. He imagined what it would be like to hold her afterwards, feeling the crispness of the blouse that encased the softness of her skin. This thought made Steve smile as he continued to watch her make her way out. He knew her blazer hung on the back of her chair at her desk where it usually was. She walked quickly and he noticed how her hair bounced from side to side. It was shorter he realized, a nice cut. She was slim, yet her skirt pulled a little tight at the back. His mind wandered to the memory of her in his bathroom that night. Even with all the commotion, he saw how beautiful she was. Her skin glowed, and he remembered well how it felt when he brushed it with his hands as he helped her put on his robe.

He dismissed these thoughts. He was sure he was too old for her. Plus, she was quickly becoming his best friend. He didn't want to do anything to destroy that again. He consoled himself with the fact that she never had to know he felt about her in this way. Only natural, he supposed.

As if she could read his thoughts, she stopped, looked back over her shoulder at him, gave a puzzled smiled, and continued on her way.

Once she was out of sight, he forced himself to think of some-thing else. Again, he wracked his brain trying to figure out what he had missed that night in the elevator. For the life of him, he couldn't, and it tormented him to no end. He decided after lunch he would go for a ride in the elevator. Maybe it would jog his memory. There had also been more than the usual complaints about the elevator stopping at the wrong floors, and he knew he should probably check them, anyway. He finished his lunch and left the bar. He left a tip on the table for the server.

Strolling through the lobby, he headed for the elevators.

"Steve, come here!" Penny yelled.

He was startled and a bit annoyed at the interruption. What could she want already?

Penny was waving him over frantically. She was watching one of the security screens. Curious now, he quickened his step and joined her behind the front desk.

"What is it?" he asked.

Penny put a finger to her lips and pointed to the screen. There were Alec and Carla, having a conversation in the hallway on the third floor. Steve picked up right away that Alec was furious. Carla, on the other hand, appeared very upset. Carla was doing most of the talking. Alec was attempting to calm her down. He even put his hand on her shoulder. It would have been a kind gesture had his eyes not been filled with so much anger. Alec was nodding his head, yes, repeatedly as Carla spoke. Her speech was very animated, with her arms and hands following along. Then she must have said something to enrage him even more. He stopped trying to calm her. He glared at her, his face so close to hers they were almost touching. He was shaking his head, NO. This response escalated Carla's mood, and tears rolled down her cheeks. With a look of exasperation, Alec wiped away the tears with his thumb. For some unknown reason this made her angry. She flipped his hands away from her face, and then to Penny and Steve's amazement, she began pounding on his chest with both fists. Alec grabbed her wrists and held them together firmly. He leaned over and spoke right into her face. Of course, they couldn't make out what he had said. They did know it was bad when Carla began to tremble. Alec pushed her away and walked slowly down the hallway. Carla ran in the other direction, face in her hands.

"Well! What do you think of my motive theory now?" asked Penny.

"Never doubt a woman's intuition."

"You better go. We'll talk later."

Steve headed back in the direction of the elevator to check them out as planned. He pressed the button and waited. He could see on the light display above that it had stopped on the second floor. The doors finally opened and out walked Alec, his face red.

"Hey, Alec, how's it going?"

"Not great."

"Anything I can do?" asked Steve.

"Just your job for a change!" Alec barked.

Steve might have been offended had he not just witnessed the scene with Carla. He knew he did his job well and he knew Alec knew it too—just displaced anger.

Steve entered and pressed the button for five. If he was going to ride the elevator to check it out, he figured he might as well stop at his room and brush his teeth. Standing in the elevator, he noticed that the plywood that covered the wall of the elevator where the mirrored glass had shattered had still not been replaced. He wondered if anyone would ever fix it. The maintenance guy might be slow, but he eventually got things done. Not this time, though. Steve figured the guy didn't have the heart to do it. Either that or he was scared. He had noticed the maintenance guy blowing his nose several times at the funeral, trying to stifle a tear. He must have been fond of Natalie. He was a long-time employee and likely knew her parents and remembered her as a child. He was obviously shaken by her death.

Looking at the plywood, Steve considered that it was one thing for the maintenance guy not to get it fixed, but he was surprised Alec had let it go this long. The man was more likely to get rid of the constant reminder, or at least worry what the guests would think, but even Alec had ignored the repair delay. Maybe he believed that replacing the plywood with a new mirror would make the completely grisly event too real. It would seem as though they had accepted the tragedy and decided to move on, even without Nat. Steve made a note to ask Alec if it would be OK if he called in someone to come fix it. Everyone would do better without this constant reminder.

The elevator stopped at the third floor. Here we go, he thought. He was surprised to find someone actually waiting to get on. It was a guest. A conference was being held at the hotel that day and Steve recognized the guest as an attendee by the name tag strung around her neck.

"Oh, I'm glad to see someone on the elevator," she said. "I hear there's a ghost that rides it."

Steve smiled. "Is that so?"

The guest pressed number nine and noticed number five was already pressed.

"Will you ride with me up to the ninth floor, please?"

"Sure, but you're perfectly safe on your own. There is no ghost."

"Oh yes there is. We heard all about her from one of the maids. She said the ghost makes sure all the female guests have a wonderful stay and that all the men behave."

Steve laughed. "You should have nothing to worry about then."

The elevator stopped at the fifth floor, but Steve did not leave.

"Thank you," she said

The elevator stopped again at the seventh floor, but no one got on.

"See, that's been happening all the time. It stops and no one is there. If that's not spooky, I don't know what is."

"Just a malfunction," said Steve. "It's an old hotel, but a beauty. Did you know Winston Churchill once dined here?"

"Yes, I heard that."

The elevator doors opened on the ninth floor and the young woman thanked Steve and apologized for being such a scaredy-cat.

"No problem. You enjoy yourself, and if you have any concerns just call the front desk and ask for Steve."

"I will do that, thanks again."

The woman hurried into the ballroom, which was already filled with conference attendees. Steve frowned. He was a firm believer in punctuality and assumed she was arriving late. He pressed number five and hoped for no more interruptions.

As the elevator began its descent, Steve thought it was a relief that he only had to explain the one ghost to the lady. Apparently, and according to Randall, there were many other spirits lurking about the premises. Steve realized the stories were inevitable, considering the hotels old historic charm. The basement was supposedly full of dead souls that had never moved on, and Randall claims you can sometimes hear piano music being played late at night up on the ninth floor. He says there's no piano up there now, but at one time a rich old businesswoman, who used to rent a suite up there, owned a white piano and loved to play. At some point, she lost all her money and had to leave the hotel. It was not known where she went or what became of her. Around the same time, her white piano went missing and has never been found. Steve had actually heard it himself one time and had a tough time explaining where it came from. He knew there had to be a rational explanation. It could have been a radio playing, or a prankster trying to keep the ghost stories going. He decided he would eventually figure it out and put at least one ghost story to rest.

The elevator stopped on the seventh floor and he was surprised again to see someone waiting for it. He realized he should be more surprised when it stopped for no one, but that happened more often than not. It was Carla waiting to get on with her cart. Her eyes were still red, but she smiled at him demurely. He offered to help manoeuvre her cart onboard, but she said she could manage. He stood against the door to hold it from closing as she wheeled it in. As she squeezed past him, the front of her body brushed his, her full breasts, barely contained in her uniform, pressing into his chest as she slid by. He wondered if this was done on purpose, then decided no, it couldn't be. He was surprised she had smiled at him though, instead of her usual sneer.

"Thank you for holding the door," she said, as it closed.

"No problem, Carla," he said. Without realizing it, he was looking down at her breasts and she noticed and smiled. Steve looked away and thought to himself that he should probably start dating or something. He was worried he would end up a dirty old man. Carla pressed the lobby button as it stopped on Steve's floor. He nodded politely to her as he exited.

That was strange, he thought. Carla not only being civil to him, but also actually being nice?

Chapter 21

Penny couldn't wait for her shift to end. She was anxious to talk to Steve about what they had seen on the security camera. She still had an hour left, and the hands on the clock barely seemed to move, no matter how many times she checked.

All afternoon she had been overflowing with excitement. What they saw proved that Alec and Carla had a relationship. That should be enough to discount the alibi Carla made up to protect him, and it would also secure a motive—enough to reopen the case and at least have Alec taken in for questioning, if not arrested and charged with murder on the spot.

She had carefully saved the tape of the scene and made a copy, which she placed in the safe. Then she watched it over and over again. She surmised that perhaps Carla couldn't live with the guilt over lying about Alec being with her. He had probably forced her to say it. On the other hand, maybe something had spooked her.

"Maybe Carla knows that Steve and I suspect Alec," she said to herself. "And she's afraid to be implicated if he's caught. Maybe she was telling Alec all this, and it made him really mad."

Penny imagined several scenarios. All pointed to Alec being guilty of murder. She knew it must be so. She was sure Steve was convinced now, too. Watching the tape again, she decided Carla must have told Alec she was going to the police. She would recant the alibi she made up. Tell them all about their relationship. That was probably when Alec became furious. Yes, thought Penny; that makes the most sense. Maybe he'd even threatened Carla's life, too. She hoped the police would have a way to make out what was said. Surely a lip reader would be able to tell.

Penny could barely wait to tell Steve her theories. Still glued to the screen, she never noticed Carla standing quietly at the desk. Penny jumped when she saw her.

"Sorry," Carla said. "I didn't mean to startle you"

In a panic, Penny began pressing buttons to stop the tape, praying that Carla had not noticed what she was watching.

"That's OK," she said, smiling too big a smile. "What do you need?"

"I was looking for Steve."

"Is there a security concern?"

"No, I just needed to ask him something."

"I don't have any idea where he is. I could call his cell for you."

"No, thanks. I'll see him later."

Carla slowly pushed her cart to the elevator.

That's weird, thought Penny. Steve always said Carla didn't like him. Wonder what she wants him for?

She decided not to risk watching the tape anymore. What if Alec happened by! He would walk right behind the desk. She ejected the tape and put it in her purse. Her shift was almost over. She decided she would head straight up to Steve's room as soon as she was done. He would know what to do. She was sure he'd be in his room, but just in case she sent him a text from the computer: 'meet u in 503, 15 min'.

....

Steve, his shift over, was in his room enjoying a relaxing shower. He had never replaced the mirror that Penny cut her toe on. He decided he never would. He had just finished shaving and was standing with his eyes closed, letting the warm water pulsate on his back. He had left the bathroom door open and could hear the 40s hits playing in the other room. He felt good, and his mind drifted as the water washed over him.

His cell phone beeped. It sounded like another one of those stupid text messages. He wanted to ignore it, but worried it could be important. He turned the water off and stepped out onto the mat. Reaching for a towel, he dried himself quickly, walked out of the bathroom, and picked up his cell from the bedside table. He flipped it open and read the message. Penny was coming up in 15 minutes.

He was glad he had got out to read it. He went in the washroom and quickly combed his hair. He had just slipped on a fresh pair of boxers when he heard the knock at the door. She's early, he thought.

"Come on in Pen, its open."

"Steve?"

It was not Penny's voice.

He grabbed his housecoat off the hook of the bathroom door and put it on. Penny had returned it freshly laundered. Tying the belt tightly he walked out of the bathroom.

He couldn't have been more surprised to see Carla standing in his room. He blushed, embarrassed to be caught in such a personal state by this woman he barely knew. However, once he saw her distraught look he forgot all about it. He noticed her large eyes were red and looked as though tears might well up any moment.

He apologized for his appearance. "Sorry, I thought you were someone else."

"I need your help."

A tear rolled down her cheek and Steve pulled a tissue from the box and handed it to her.

"Thank you."

He sat on the edge of the bed and patted the spot beside him. He couldn't help but notice a button had popped open on the front of her uniform, exposing a view he did his best to ignore.

"Not many chairs in here," he said. "Why do you need my help?"

She never hesitated, just said it directly. "Alec murdered his wife. He knows I know, and I'm scared."

Steve was blown away. He and Penny had suspected it, but in the back of his mind, he still hoped Alec hadn't done it. At times, he had deluded himself into thinking it really could have been a freak accident.

As if the sky had reacted to Carla's announcement, heavy rain began to pelt the window. Lightning lit the sky, and a crack of thunder made them both jump. The radio stopped playing. After a brief moment of silence, Steve spoke softly. "How do you know Alec did this?"

"He made me say he was with me. I didn't want to lie, but what else could I do?"

"You didn't have to do anything! Why didn't you tell the police? Or me? We could have helped."

"He's my boss, and there are other reasons. He's been making me do a lot of things I don't want to do, for a long time."

At this admission, she began to weep uncontrollably. Steve put one arm around her shoulder to comfort her.

"Oh Steve!" In one quick motion she pressed her full lips hard on his mouth, and pressed her chest tightly against his. Both her hands held the back of his head, and she ran her fingers through his hair.

He was too startled to react before the door slammed open and Penny glared at them in horror and disbelief. She stood frozen, mouth gaping, tape in hand.

Steve stood up and almost wanted to cry himself when he saw the look on Penny's face. He realized for the first time that, even if she didn't know it herself, Penny had feelings for him, too.

Another realization hit him hard. He could scarcely believe it, but he knew now that it was the truth.

Carla sat on the edge of the bed, not looking at either of them. As if noticing it for the very first time, she looked down at the button on her uniform that had come undone. She chose that inopportune moment to fasten it. Penny noticed, took one last look at Steve, and slammed the door shut behind her.

Chapter 22

That stupid bitch! Alec had retreated to his office on the fourth floor shortly after his run-in with Carla. He was furious. He paced back and forth in the large carpeted area in front of his desk. The weather outside his window matched his mood. As the storm accelerated, so did his anger. He picked up the crystal egg paperweight Nat had given him for their first anniversary and hurled it across the room. It smashed to pieces, which only infuriated him more.

A crack of lightning flashed across the sky. He was so relieved when Carla had supplied his alibi. They both knew that without it, he would certainly be implicated, if not found guilty, in Nat's death. He had motive, for sure. Add opportunity and he was going away for a long time.

It had been deemed an accident, and except for some idle gossip, he was in the clear. Now, Carla was going to ruin everything. Why had he trusted her? Today she had told him she wanted to recant her statement. Tell the truth. Said she couldn't lie about it anymore. What a pile of crap. He knew the real reason.

He wished now he had never set eyes on her, let alone hired her. He should have listened to Nat. It was a mistake and he could see that now. In the beginning, it seemed like a good idea. She would be the perfect employee, indebted to him for giving her the job. He had argued with Nat, claimed he felt sorry for her and wanted to help her out. In reality, he liked the idea of her being indebted to him.

He began to pace faster, avoiding the broken glass from the crystal egg. The storm continued to strengthen, and he hoped the power would hold out.

All spilled milk now, he thought. The important thing was to figure out what he had to do and soon. Carla had to be stopped. He hoped the strong warning he had given her today was enough to hold her off, but for how long? What would it take to shut her up for good? God, how he hated her. She was ruining everything.

"What am I going to do? What am I going to do," he repeated as he paced.

Chapter 23

Penny stood alone in the hallway outside Steve's room. Her head was whirling and she had to steady herself by holding onto the wall. You're not going to faint today, she told herself.

Standing up straight, she dug deep into her core and willed herself to be strong. She was furious. Not that she had any claim on Steve. They were just friends. Technically, he had done nothing wrong, except lie to her, which was much worse. She was getting madder by the second. Yes, that was it. He had lied to her, saying Carla wouldn't give him the time of day. Hah! What a joke! And him not the least bit interested. Yeah, right!

She had trusted him and he had lied. It had probably been going on for some time. She was so wrapped up in solving Nat's murder that she hadn't even noticed. That was another blow. Now that she had proof Alec's alibi was a sham, something had to be done. She had counted on Steve to help her confront Alec. What an idiot she had been. Again.

The lights in the hallway flickered, and she felt a cool soft breeze whisk by her. Then the hallway went dark and she thought she could hear footsteps. She shivered and wrapped her arms around herself tightly. The lights came back on and she knew what she had to do. She felt strong, confident. She decided at that moment that she would never again be a victim of a man's deceits. She thought of Edith and Natalie. Both of them had suffered the ultimate deception. Their lives cut short by the very men they loved and trusted.

Heading for the stairwell, she clung hard to the tape in her pocket. She practically flew down the stairs to the fourth floor. It was time Alec found out that she wasn't about to let him get away with murder.

Meanwhile, Steve felt physically sick, sick all the way to his stomachs core. He never wanted to see that look of hurt on Penny's face ever again. He knew where Penny was headed, and he had to stop her.

Ignoring Carla, who still sat on the edge of his bed, sniffling and dabbing her eyes, he grabbed his uniform pants and shirt and threw them on quickly. He opened the top drawer of his dresser, hesitated a moment, then retrieved his gun and jammed it in the back of his pants.

"Let's go."

"Where Steve? Where are we going? I'm so scared."

Steve didn't have time for this. He grabbed her by the wrist, pulled her off the bed and dragged her out the door with him.

She yanked her wrist out of his hand. "I'm coming."

Without speaking another word to each other, they quickly descended the stairs to the fourth floor. Carla followed obediently, trying her best to keep up with him. She knew where they were headed and was glad. Boy, would Alec be surprised. She smiled contently.

Penny hadn't knocked when she reached the door to Alec's office. She hadn't entered quietly, either. She turned the knob and swung the door open with all her strength. It banged loudly against the wall.

Alec took one look at her and was stunned. This was not the Penny he knew. She looked enraged and determined. Trying to cover his own rage, and in an attempt to diffuse hers, he smiled pleasantly.

"Penny! What a surprise! You don't visit me up here often enough. Isn't your shift over? What can I help you with?"

"Shut up, you lying bastard!" she shouted. "I know you murdered your wife and I can prove it."

He noticed the tape in her hand and glared at her.

"You don't know what you're talking about."

"Like hell I don't."

He wanted to grab her by the throat and stop her from saying anything more. He could barely hide his rage, but knew he had to.

"How dare you! I loved Natalie. I could never hurt her..."

"Loved her to death, maybe? I know all about your affair with Carla. Once the authorities see this tape they'll know too."

Alec's eyes narrowed.

"Remember your little lover's spat earlier this afternoon? Well it's all on here." Penny held up the tape. "No one will believe that stupid alibi she made up for you after they see this."

Penny was astounded at how she was handling this. She felt in control and confident, and she was enjoying it.

"Penny, the police proved it was an accident. The case is closed. You do have a vivid imagination. I'll give you that. Are you getting enough sleep? You look tired. Now why don't you just give me that tape and let's forget all about this."

Alec held out his hand for the tape. Penny noticed his hand was quivering.

"I will not. It's time you paid for what you did, and I'm going to make sure you do."

Alec knew that if the authorities saw the tape they'd reopen the case. They'd quickly conclude that he had motive and opportunity. He walked slowly toward her.

Oh my God, thought Penny. He's going to kill me, too. Why did I come here alone? I need Steve! All her confidence was gone, replaced with true terror. She edged backwards towards the door, but he came too quickly. She was no match for him. He was physically much stronger. He tried to grab the tape, but she held it close. He grabbed both her shoulders. His fingers dug into her skin, hurting her. He began to shake her.

"Give me that tape. Now!"

"Nooo!" she screamed.

Steve suddenly barged into the room, with Carla in tow. He drew his gun, and holding it with both hands, pointed it at Alec. Carla gasped and began to edge out the door. Without looking back at her Steve demanded, "Don't you go anywhere, Carla."

"Help me, Steve. Please help me," Penny pleaded.

Alec seized Penny, holding her in front of him like a shield.

"What are you going to do, Stevie? Shoot me? I hear it's your specialty, judge and jury, all wrapped into one."

Steve was caught off guard. He had no idea Alec knew anything about Jim.

"This time you're wrong, Stevie. I never killed anyone, and I don't care what your little girlfriend here thinks she knows."

As he spoke, Alec manoeuvred himself and Penny toward the door.

"You killed her!" Carla screamed. "You know you did, and I won't lie for you anymore."

Alec gave her a look of disgust, and then ignored her. His back was to the door, and he was still holding Penny in front of him. Steve and Carla had moved in an arc and were in the room, facing the door. Steve never took his eyes off them, and he had not lowered his gun.

Alec was scared to death. He had never had a gun pointed at him in his whole life. Everything he had worked so hard for was crumbling around him. Now it had all come down to this one moment. He had to get out of there. Then he'd have to run. He'd go so far away no one would ever find him or hear from him again. But how?

A loud crack of lightning offered his opportunity. Steve was momentarily distracted, and that was when Alec pushed Penny hard in Steve's direction. Then Alec ran.

Time stood still. As Penny hurtled toward him, Steve saw
Jimmy's face, not hers. She slammed against him, right on his
gun, and then fell to the floor. She lay motionless. Steve dropped
his gun and fell to the floor beside her.

Carla yelled frantically, "He's getting away!"

Steve didn't care. "Oh God, Penny, I'm so sorry"

"Get him!" she yelled. But it wasn't Carla, this time. It was
Penny. "Don't let him get away."

It was at that moment that reality set in. The gun had not gone
off. It never even had bullets in it. He had never had the heart to
load it since Jimmy died. His mind was playing tricks on him.

"You OK, Pen?"

"Yeah! Now go!"

He ran into the hallway just in time to see the elevator doors
close. He ran down the stairs down to the lobby.

In the meantime, Penny ran to Alec's desk and called the police.
She asked for Chief Dan.

"We need help at the Marlborough Hotel. A murderer is on the
loose. Steve has gone after him."

When she hung up, she looked at Carla.

"Come with me."

When they arrived in the lobby, Steve was on his cell. Two officers
were already arriving at the front door, and Randall was pointing
them in the direction of the elevators.

"Where is he?" asked Penny.

"You won't believe this," he said. "He's stuck in the elevator
between floors. The storm must have cut the power."

Penny smiled at him, forgetting how mad she had been earlier.
She decided that it was no accident Alec was caught in the elevator. The storm wasn't to blame. She knew Edith had had a hand
in this and it made her smile even more.

Carla walked up to Steve and put her hand on his arm.

"I'm so relieved. You were magnificent, Steve."

"Wasn't anything I did," he said, looking sheepishly at Penny.

The officers arrived at the elevators and tried to take charge of a situation they knew nothing about. It was obvious to everyone who was really in charge.

"No need to draw your guns gentlemen," Steve told them. "He's not armed. Maintenance is on the way to get him out."

Steve was amused to see the maintenance man shuffling quickly through the lobby, crowbar in hand. Randall was close behind him.

"Stand back, everybody," said Steve, as the doors were pried open.

Penny was surprised to see Steve help Alec out of the elevator. Steve even told him to watch his head. She couldn't believe Steve would be so nice after all that had happened, when likely she'd have banged Alec's head a few times.

How apropos, she thought, the murderer trapped in the very elevator where he committed the murder.

Alec stood quietly, ready to accept his fate.

"What the hell went on here, Steve?" asked Chief Dan.

"Well, it appears your detectives made a grave mistake. Natalie Kent's death was no accident. She was murdered. True, that night the elevator did jolt to a stop, causing Natalie to lose her footing and bang her head. The mirror did break, but the shard of the glass did not accidentally meet with her throat. It was plunged in by the hand of a killer."

All eyes shifted to Alec, who squirmed. Penny looked at him with disdain. Carla stood with her arms folded across her chest, with an I-told-you-so look on her face.

Then, with a great deal of satisfaction, Steve pointed at Carla. "Arrest her."

All eyes shifted to Carla in disbelief. Carla's arms dropped and she lowered her eyes. She looked as if she wanted to disappear. Alec looked confused, then enraged.

"Are you kidding?" asked Chief Dan. "On what grounds?"

"For starters, she's an illegal alien, working without a visa. Dig a little deeper and I'm sure you'll be able to charge her with the murder of Natalie Kent."

Penny was incredulous. Had Steve lost it? Carla never killed Natalie. It was Alec. She was very confused.

The officers didn't seem to know what to do. They didn't know Steve. They wondered why this hotel security guard was in charge, and even more confusing, Chief Dan was letting him.

"Put the cuffs on her boys. Take her down to the station. I'll meet you there. Steve, you'd better come along. You too, Mr. Kent," ordered Chief Dan.

"I'm coming, too," Penny said.

Chief Dan looked at Steve as if to say, who is she?

"Sure, Penny, of course. You come, too," Steve said.

Randall was back at the front desk. He had watched the final drama unfold from a safe distance. Steve would fill him in on the details later. Someone had to stay to take care of the hotel and her guests.

Chapter 24

Carla was taken away in the patrol car. Chief Dan drove Alec, Steve, and Penny in his car. Alec rode in the front with Chief Dan. Steve and Penny sat in the back. Steve noticed that Penny looked pale. He put his arm around her shoulders.

"It's OK now. Everything is going to be OK."

Chief Dan and Alec exchanged surprised glances.

"Before we get to the station, tell me what we have on this girl, Steve," Chief Dan said.

Both Penny and Alec looked at Steve.

"Sorry, Alec, but I really was beginning to believe you were guilty," Steve said. "It all pointed in that direction. When I saw the security footage of you and Carla arguing, it was pretty convincing."

"What changed your mind?" asked Alec.

Steve looked apologetically at Penny. "It was when Carla came to my room tonight. She was awfully upset. She claimed the alibi she gave was all lies, and she wanted to come clean. She pointed the finger at you, Alec. Said you killed Natalie and forced her to make up an alibi for you. What were you two arguing about in the hallway, anyway?"

"She said she was going to recant her statement, tell them she lied to help me. I never asked her to do it. When she did, I figured things were looking bad for me. Without an alibi, people might think I could have actually done it. I had lost enough and wasn't about to lose the hotel and spend the rest of my life in jail. I could never have hurt Natalie. I loved her. It wasn't a perfect marriage, but I loved her."

"Loved her!" Penny cried. "You hypocrite. If you loved her so much, why were you having an affair with Carla?"

"I never was. I told Steve that. There were many opportunities. Carla was forever coming on to me. I told Natalie all about it. We didn't have secrets. That's why Natalie hated her so much, wanted me to fire her. I couldn't fire her, though. I felt sorry for her. She sent money home and her family needed it."

Penny couldn't believe it. Could she have misjudged him so badly?

Chief Dan said, "Back to the facts, Steve. What's going to bring this case to a close?"

"Well, there had been something nagging at me, something I missed. Penny, you helped figure it out. It was when you said there was a bright light in the elevator where Natalie was lying. It got me thinking. Then it all came to me in my room when Carla kissed me." Steve smiled, "You were right Penny. She does smell like vinegar."

Penny shifted uncomfortably in her seat. Steve instinctively removed his arm from her shoulder.

"Go on," Chief Dan urged.

"Anyway, the mirrors in the elevator were never that clean. I suspect the cleaning staff didn't like to spend much time in them because of all the ghost stories. I finally realized the light coming from the elevator was the reflection of the light hitting the shard of mirror—sorry Alec—sticking in Nat's throat. It had to have been just cleaned to reflect such a bright light. Now I know the detectives found no fingerprints on the glass. That's because Carla cleaned them off after jabbing the shard into her throat."

Penny looked as if she was going to throw up, and Alec looked stricken.

"When Carla kissed me tonight, I could smell vinegar. I realized that's what I had been forgetting. That night, the elevator smelled of vinegar. That's when I knew Carla had done it. I'm sure, Dan, if you check that piece of mirror again you'll find traces of vinegar."

"And Carla was allergic to cleaning products," Penny said.
Steve nodded. "Exactly."

"She was the only one who used vinegar for cleaning," Alec said. "And it contained a few other ingredients, too. I can call Randall and get him to retrieve her spray bottle for evidence."

"We'll have an officer go do that, but thanks," said Chief Dan. "What was her motive?"

"That should be obvious," Penny replied. "She wanted Alec all to herself. Plus, Natalie wanted her fired."

Steve smiled and returned his arm around her shoulder.

"You're becoming quite the detective. She actually implicated herself when she decided to recant your alibi, Alec. What she succeeded in doing was destroying an alibi that would have worked for her, too. Any idea why she'd do that?"

Penny piped up too quickly, "Unrequited love!"

Alec lowered his head into his hands and looked as if he might cry.

"Yes, you're probably right," Alec sighed. "After Natalie died, Carla's advances became more insistent. She even mentioned marriage, for God's sake. Poor Natalie. If only I had listened to her and fired Carla like she wanted. You know the fight you have on tape in the hallway? The reason Carla changed her mind about the alibi was because I rejected her. She thought I was in love with her. I admit I might have led her on a bit after she made up the alibi for me. I didn't want to upset her. But she wanted more than promises. Who knows, maybe she wanted to be Natalie. Maybe she mistook my kindness towards her for more than it was. I was such a fool, and Natalie paid the price."

They drove in silence for the rest of the trip. Penny moved closer and put her head on Steve's shoulder. She would never ask Steve about the scene in his room with Carla. She trusted him completely.

When they arrived at the station Chief Dan said, "Good work Steve. We need you back you know, whether you think you're ready or not."

Chapter 25

It had been quite a night. At 5 a.m. Steve finally decided to leave, and borrowed Dan's car to drive Penny home. Penny was very tired. It seemed the coffee never quit flowing at the station, but she could only drink so much of the stuff. The coffee and adrenaline that had kept her awake this long was slowly wearing off. Steve, on the other hand, was hopping. He drank coffee like water, one after the other. It was very tough on him not being part of the questioning Carla was undergoing.

Carla chose to waive her rights to legal representation. Why did she need a lawyer if she was innocent, she told them. It had been a long night of questioning that had eventually worn Carla down. At first she played the victim. She threw accusation after accusation at Alec. She started by claiming he had raped her several times. He threatened to fire her and even kill her if she recanted her alibi, which she said he forced her to give in the first place. Worst of all, she said, he murdered his wife. She told a compelling story about how Alec had let her in on his plan, then bragged afterward about killing Natalie. She said she was too afraid of him to tell anyone about his plan. Instead, she convinced herself it was just talk; that he could never go through with it. She began to cry when she told the detectives that he did it for the money, for the hotel, and for her. He wanted it all. When she refused to marry him, he went wild. That's when she knew she needed help and turned to Steve.

Chief Dan and Steve watched the whole drama through a two-way mirror. Alec and Penny had to wait in the small cafeteria.

Steve couldn't believe how convincing Carla could be. He and Chief Dan could both tell the detectives were falling for it. Steve asked Dan if he could please go in and talk to her.

"I wish I could let you Steve, but you're not on the payroll. It would blow any chances of prosecuting her if it ever leaked."

"Yeah, I know. It's just so damn frustrating."

The two detectives came out of the room. They glared at Steve.

One of them said, "Chief, I think she's telling the truth. We're questioning the wrong person."

The other one added, "We need to talk to Alec."

"You will boys, later," said Chief Dan. "Right now, I want you to go back in there. I was watching her, and she tells a good story. Try a little harder. I bet the details of her story will start to get a little sketchy."

One detective sighed and the other shook his head. They both poured fresh coffee into their cups and went back into the interrogation room. One of them had taken a bottled water from the fridge. He opened it and gave it to Carla. She smiled through her tears and thanked him.

As Dan had predicted, Carla's story had subtle changes the next time she told it. But the detectives had been forewarned. They caught the discrepancies and took her to task. The more she tried to explain, the worse it got. She was getting tired. Steve knew a person could tell the truth over and over again, no matter how tired they got. Stringing a pack of lies became increasingly difficult when one was weak from lack of sleep.

It got so bad she finally had to change her story completely. She knew full well the shard of glass that had been plunged into Natalie's throat would carry traces of her trademark cleaning solution. She also had to make excuses for her earlier lies. In her usual style, she played her next angle with dramatic flair. It was her last kick at the can. If she was going down, so was Alec.

"OK," she screamed. "I did it. I did it. He made me! He threatened my life!"

"Now we're getting somewhere," Steve told Dan.

It was just after 4 a.m. when Carla finally caved in. She could see there was no way out and she was tired. She admitted to everything except planning it. She spoke of her conversation in the elevator with Natalie that night. She told how Natalie ordered her to leave her husband alone and called her a bad name. Carla said she hated Natalie. She was such a bitch. Thought she was so much better than me.

Then Carla admitted how she was in love with Alec. Said Natalie didn't deserve him. How he deserved someone who would love him and cater to him, like she would. She knew he loved her too, but couldn't act on it because of Natalie. Carla said their argument escalated and Natalie got so mad she fired her right there in the elevator. Said if her husband wasn't man enough to tell Carla she was through, she would.

With her head down, Carla continued.

"Just like that she fired me. I was furious. I could actually see red. Then the elevator jolted and the lights went out. Natalie must have fallen back and hit the mirror, causing it to shatter. The lights came on a second later and I saw her lying there, unconscious. I was still angry, but more than anything, I was scared. Where would I go? In an instant, the solution came to me. It was the hand of fate. I picked up a piece of the broken mirror and plunged it into her throat. Then, realizing my fingerprints would be on it, I grabbed my cleaning bottle and cloth and quickly wiped them off. The elevator stopped at the next floor and it was still dark from the power outage. Again, this was fate, offering me the opportunity to escape unseen. I ran into one of the vacant rooms and called Alec, said I needed help. He never showed up."

No one spoke. Then Carla added, "She never knew what happened. There was no struggle."

Carla left out the part about the cut she had sustained on her hand after stabbing Natalie. Why add fuel to the fire, she had thought. She knew the blood from her cut had dripped and mixed with Natalie's blood near the wound. At the time, no one had noticed, and no one had thought to look. She had not been a suspect, not even a person of interest. She held her left hand over the slight scar on her right hand. This had become a habit since that night. She was terrified that someone would notice and become suspicious. It was almost a relief to confess, but she feared what the future would hold. Would she be tried here or extradited to her own country? She hoped for the former.

"I would like to call a lawyer now."

....

Steve drove Penny out Portage Avenue to her parents' home in St. James.

"I still can't believe it," she said.

"Things aren't always as they seem, Pen."

"I was so sure it was Alec. It all fit so neatly."

"Sometimes that's a bad sign," he said. "If it's too neat and orderly, it's likely not right."

"True, I guess."

"Aren't you going to ask me about my kissing Carla?"

"Nope, no need. You're off the hook."

Steve smiled. He had a strong urge to stop the car at the moment and take her into his arms. However, he could see they were nearing her parent's house. All the lights were on and they were watching out the picture window for her.

Penny laughed. "They still think I'm a kid. I'm going to have to get my own place."

"You can't blame them for worrying after the night we've had."

"No, you're right."

"Not a kid, eh? How old are you, Pen?"

"A lady never tells, but rest assured, older than you think. Sun block and hats not only keep the freckles from taking over, they stave off those nasty wrinkles. You should try them," she laughed and got out of the car.

Steve smiled and shook his head. I don't know what I see in that woman, he thought.

After making sure she got in OK, he went straight back to the station to see how things were going. He found Chief Dan waiting outside for him. Dan was ready to go home for some much-needed shuteye. Steve threw him his keys and went into the station. He found Alec sound asleep in the cafeteria, head resting on his arms on the table. He gently woke him and they shared a cab back to the hotel. Alec spoke first.

"I'm real sorry, Steve."

"For what?" said Steve, looking sideways at him. The adrenaline that had kept him going all night had subsided. He was growing more and more tired.

"You know, for pushing Penny at you in my office. I panicked."

"Well, you thought I might shoot you for a murder you didn't commit."

"I know how I suffered when I lost Nat. I still suffer and miss her. It's so bad I can't eat or function half the time. I would never forgive myself if anything had happened to Penny. It's obvious how much you two care for each other."

The comment surprised Steve. He didn't realize it was so obvious to anyone. He was also seeing a side of Alec he had never seen before, and he liked it.

"Pen and I are just friends, for now. And just be thankful I never put any bullets in that gun."

"No bullets? I wish I'd known. What a relief. So Penny was never in any danger, and come to think of it neither was I."

"Things aren't always as they appear," said Steve, for the second time that night. "Sometimes the things you don't see are more important than the things you do."

It was then that he made a decision to do something first thing in the morning.

"I have no idea what you're talking about, but you're a good man, Steve."

"So are you, Alec."

The storm had subsided and the rain had stopped. The air in the cab was stale but they kept their windows closed as the driver sped through large puddles on the street.

Finally, Steve was back in his room and glad to be by himself. It seemed like ages since Carla had been there. He stripped down, not even bothering to hang up his uniform, letting it fall to the floor, and went straight to bed. His dreams were a mish-mash of images. First, he dreamt of Edith. She was looking for something. On Edith's ears were shiny diamond earrings. Then, Edith turned into Natalie, who was looking in a hand mirror, fixing her hair. She paused and looked at Steve and smiled. Then Natalie began washing the mirror, her hair turned dark, and she was Carla, smashing the mirror. Steve tried to stop her but she was out of reach. He tossed and turned in his bed. Then they were all gone and it was Jim, not Alec, holding Penny in front of him as a shield. Jim was laughing and Penny was crying and yelling, "Shoot him, kill him, please save me." He did what she said and Jim fell to the ground. Beside him lay Sidney. Then he was in a back lane. Someone was calling to him. "Steve, up here." He looked and saw Sidney on the fire escape. She was waving and smiling. Then another voice was calling to him. Who was it?

"Steve, wake up."

He opened his eyes, looked up, and saw Penny.

"It's past noon. You wouldn't answer your phone. Are you coming for lunch?"

He smiled. Had she actually come into work after the night they had?

"Yeah, I'm coming."

After lunch, he walked over to the Portage Place mall. When he reached the store he wanted, he deliberated for some time before making his final choice, then headed straight to the cashier and made his purchase.

He walked back to the hotel, swinging the bag that held his purchase. The sun was shining and the streets smelled fresh from last night's rain. He could hardly wait to show Penny what he had bought.

As soon as he entered the front doors of the hotel, he noticed Randall and Penny at the front desk. Great, he thought. Randall was early. Penny's shift wasn't over for a bit but he wanted her to come with him.

"Hey Randall," he said. "Penny fill you in on the night's antics."

"You bet. Unbelievable! Penny promised you'd both come for dinner with the wife and me tonight. She's been dying to meet you two after all the stories I've told her. We can talk all about it then. Is Rae & Jerry's OK?"

Penny looked apologetic. "I hope you don't mind, Steve."

"Mind? How could I? Our first date, a perfect double! It is a date, right, Penny?"

"Yeah, I guess."

"Well you don't have to gush," said Steve. He laughed and so did Randall.

"Could you come with me, Penny?" said Steve. "I need to show you something."

Randall motioned for her to go.

They took the elevator, which stopped at only one unscheduled stop where no one was waiting.

"Not bad," Penny observed as they got out on Steve's floor. "What's in the bag?"

"It's what I want to show you."

They entered his room and he quickly removed a box from the bag. He lifted the lid and pulled out a brand new pair of shoes. They were dark brown, shiny, and each had a buckle.

"Oh! Steve!"

Penny picked up the shoes and admired them.

"They're for Edith, aren't they?"

"This doesn't mean I believe in ghosts, but I thought they would make you happy."

"Oh they do. But I'm sure they'll make Edith a lot happier."

He lifted a floorboard by the dresser, placed the shoes inside, and carefully replaced the board.

"No one will ever find them there, except Edith."

"Oh so you do believe in ghosts?"

"You know what I meant."

Steve went with her on her way back to the front desk. He knew she wouldn't have wanted to ride the elevator alone. Their ride down went smoothly, with no unscheduled stops.

"Told you," said Penny.

When they reached the front desk, Steve said he had to go out again.

"Where now?"

Steve was almost out the front door when he called back. "To see Chief Dan. I'm going back if they'll have me."

Excited with the news she chased him out the door and called after him. "Really, that's great! It's where you belong, you know."

Steve stopped and walked back towards her. He reached for her face and held her chin gently with his hand. He lifted her face to his and kissed her. They held the kiss a long time, unaware of those on the street who stopped to stare. He dropped his hand from her chin, stepped back from her, and started to sing one of the old 40s hits, "I'll be seeing you. . ."

He twirled on one heel and walked away, paused, looked back, and tipped an imaginary hat towards her.

She laughed. "You bet you will! Pick me up at seven, and don't be late."

Epilogue

She watched them as they carefully placed the shoes under the loose floorboard. It was the nice man who looked so handsome in his uniform. The pretty lady was with him. She knew he was going to help her; he had such kind eyes.

She had become so used to him staying in her room that she barely bothered with him at all. She only visited him in his dreams.

They had both admired the shoes before they gave them to her, and so had she. They were perfect. Not exactly like the ones she had purchased for her trip to Vancouver, but close, perhaps even better. She was free. Now she could finally leave this dreary room for the last time.

She sensed someone else in the room with her. She looked and saw the elderly lady who played the white piano.

"Come, Edith. We can both go now."

Edith smiled and took her hand. They drifted away together.

The End